D0393876

WHITE WIDOW

JIM LEHRER

WHITE

WIDOW

RANDOM HOUSE

NEW YORK

Library of Congress Cataloging-in-Publication Data
Lehrer, James.
White Widow / Jim Lehrer.—1st ed.
p.   cm.
ISBN 0-679-45236-2
I. Title.
PS3562.E4419M37   1996   813'.54—dc20   96-1877

Random House website address: http://www.randomhouse.com/

Printed in the United States of America on acid-free paper
Book design by J. K. Lambert
9 8 7 6 5 4 3 2
First Edition

For the bus people

WHITE   WIDOW

*J*ack saw immediately that she was a White Widow. He knew even before she was right there in front of him, when she was still in line with seven or eight other passengers ahead of her. It was the hair that first made her stand out. It was dark brown and long and it fell down across both shoulders like an expensive shawl. She was also tall for a woman, maybe five eight. But she was thin tall.

Why was she so thin? Was she sick? Was she dying of something? Oh, no, no. She wasn't *that* thin. She was perfect thin. Thin perfect. Her face was perfect too, perfectly tanned. Had she been to the beach at Padre Island, Jack's favorite place in the world? Had she just come from being in a movie with Clark Gable?

"All the way to Corpus today, I see," he said as he took her ticket.

"That's right," she replied.

All the way to Corpus today, I see.

That's right.

She looked right at him for just a blink and then cut her eyes to her left toward the step that led up into the bus. He saw those eyes long enough to see they were the most gorgeous blue eyes he had ever seen. They reminded him of the sky over the Gulf at Padre on sunny clear days in April and May.

He had never seen a woman like her. Not in the flesh. He had the sudden desire to grab her right hand, bow forward, kiss that hand ever so gently and say, "Welcome to my chariot, White Widow of My Dreams."

Now wouldn't that be a great way to end his career with Great Western Trailways! Not even the union would defend him. It was surely against company policy for bus drivers to grab women passengers' hands and kiss them, even those of White Widows. But he could probably get away with it because nobody with the company would believe he had done such a thing. Not him. Not Jack T. Oliver, the best they had behind the wheel.

He inserted her ticket into the slot in his silver ticket punch and gave it three punches. He felt a slight quiver in his right hand as he punched. Look at that hand, he thought. What is this White Widow doing to me? He slipped the punch's ring over his right ring finger and used both hands to tear the ticket across the perforation. He handed her back the portion marked Identification Check, keeping the main section, which showed that it was a one-way ticket from Victoria, Texas, to Corpus Christi, Texas.

Why only one way? Are you never coming back?

He nodded and stepped aside and took hold of her right elbow with his right hand to guide her up into his bus.

She was wearing a cream-colored blouse that had sleeves down to just above the elbow. So he felt her skin. Only a tiny bit and only for the count of one-two. But it was like touching velvet, the kind big hotels put on lobby couches.

"Have a nice trip," he said.

"Thank you," she replied.

Have a nice trip.

Thank you.

And she disappeared up into the bus. *His* bus. He watched her turn left down the aisle to find a seat. He saw her bottom move under her skirt, a dark brown checked skirt that went just below her knees. Was it silk? He didn't know cloth that well. Most everything looked like cotton to him.

Her legs, tanned as her face, were perfectly proportioned. She was not wearing stockings. It was too hot for anybody to wear stockings. Even a White Widow.

Was that a bump there on the calf of her right leg? A bite? Had a mosquito bitten this beautiful woman's leg? Or was it more serious? Would it have to come off? Would she lose her leg?

He punched and took the tickets of the last six passengers, got them aboard and closed the bus door behind them. Twenty-six passengers in all, a good load these days. Twelve of the twenty-six were thrus from Houston. Not bad for an early September afternoon on this run, Schedule 726. Except on holidays and some summer weekends he seldom had every seat filled anymore. Only on the days before and after Christmas and Thanksgiving did he leave Houston or anywhere else with people standing in the aisle or, when the equipment was available, a second section, called a double, right behind him. Business had been slowly declining since the war ended and everybody could afford to buy a car. Some of the drivers were worried that it would eventually dry up altogether and the bus would go the way of the horse and buggy. Jack doubted that would ever happen.

He went into the bus depot to get a last call, sort out the tickets by destinations and do the paperwork.

He also hadn't said anything yet to Mr. Abernathy, who was now standing at the ticket counter with his suitcase. He was talking to Johnny Merriweather, the ticket agent on duty.

"A round-trip to Charlottesville, Virginia, please," said Mr. Abernathy. "Monticello is there and that is the home of Thomas Jefferson, the third and best president of the United States."

"Better than Ike, the one we have now?" said Johnny, playing along as everyone always did with Mr. Abernathy.

"I think General Eisenhower is making a wonderful president," Mr. Abernathy said. "I fully expect him to be reelected."

Johnny said, "I read in the *Houston Press* that some are saying he's a Communist. So's his brother."

"Please do not say things like that, please, please. I have never heard of anything like that before and I do not want to start hearing it now." Jack had never heard of anything like that before either, but he wasn't political. He simply voted Democrat like all of the other drivers and most everyone else he knew.

Johnny said, "The three o'clock to Houston that connects to Charlottesville just left, Mr. Abernathy."

"Oh, my, well, I missed it. What about the one to Mount Rushmore?"

"You missed it, too, Mr. Abernathy."

Mr. Abernathy was a small man, neatly groomed in a suit and tie. He looked to Jack to be somewhere around thirty-five, maybe forty, but it was hard to tell.

"I'm about to head off for Corpus and the Valley," Jack said. "I'm always going your way, Mr. Abernathy, and I've always got a seat for you." *Always Going Your Way* was one of the national Trailways advertising lines.

Mr. Abernathy's face turned Trailways red—crimson, they called it in company brochures. *Ride in the Crimson and Cream of a Trailways Thruliner.*

"Oh, now, I couldn't go down there. I don't have the right clothes packed. I'm ready for Mr. Jefferson in Virginia or at Mount Rushmore."

"Well, fine," said Jack. "Whenever, just remember I always have a seat for you, Mr. Abernathy."

"Yes, well, thank you. Thank you." He smiled slightly, picked up his brown leather suitcase and walked toward the main depot door.

Mr. Abernathy, a man everybody knew but nobody knew anything about, had been coming into the depot with that suitcase every month or so for years. Sometimes he just sat down and listened to the agent announce the towns on the public address system. Sometimes he just exchanged friendly words with the drivers, the agents, the porters and the others around. But occasionally he inquired about the fare to some distant and unusual place, Mount Rushmore being his usual fallback destination. A few times he even went as far as buying a ticket, but he never ever set foot on a bus. His visits were as much a part of the life in the Victoria bus depot as the tickets and the PA system.

Johnny Merriweather was a young and eager ticket agent, but his voice was all wrong for making the PA announcements. He sounded like a scared girl when he said: "All aboard for Great Western Trailways three-fifteen P.M. Silversides Air-Conditioned Thruliner to Corpus Christi and the Rio Grande Valley, now leaving from lane one . . . next to the building . . . for Inairi, Vidauri, Refugio, Woodsboro, Sinton, Odem, Calallen and Corpus Christi . . . connecting in

Corpus for Robstown, Kingsville, Alice, Falfurrias, Raymondville, Harlingen, Brownsville, McAllen, Monterrey and Mexico City . . . All aboard . . . Don't forget your baggage, please."

There had been a kid working behind the ticket counter before the war who could make those bus calls sound like they were the most important announcements in the world. A San Antonio turnaround driver, Jack's friend Paul Madison, used to say that kid's announcements were worth coming downtown to hear, just like Mr. Abernathy did sometimes. Paul Madison said they could make most anybody want to get on a bus for anywhere. The kid was on his way to being a terminal manager, and maybe someday even a district passenger agent or higher. But he went down with his ship, a minesweeper of some kind, during the Battle of Okinawa. They had a memorial service for him at the First Baptist Church in Victoria, but without his body. They never found it.

Jack did not serve in the military in either World War II or Korea because he was 4-F. An induction physical showed him not only to be overweight, which he already knew, but also to have feet and back problems that would have made him a poor soldier. The 4-F classification was a source of great embarrassment to Jack and he never spoke of it to anybody except Paul, who had been too old to go to either war.

Jack figured poor Johnny Merriweather would never get to the top at Great Western unless he did something about his voice. Which meant he had had it, because whatever voice God gave you was pretty much the voice you were stuck with all of your life.

Although Jack himself had proved it was possible to change things pretty dramatically. Just look at what had happened to him in the twelve years and four months since he became an intercity bus driver and lost seventy-two pounds. He was about to become a Master Operator, for one thing. And for another, there was that White Widow in the fifth-row left-side window seat. Until recently he could not have let his superlative imagination loose about someone like her, as he was doing now as he reboarded his bus.

There she sat, looking out the window to her left. There he stood, up in the front of the bus, facing her and the other passengers. He was ready to make his welcome-aboard announcement.

A sour splash of his vegetable-soup-with-saltines lunch rushed into his mouth. His right leg started shaking uncontrollably and he felt sweat on his face and on the top of his head under his uniform cap.

It was the White Widow. She wasn't even looking at him. But there she was.

Forget the announcement, Jack. Just go over and sit down behind the steering wheel and drive this thing away from here before you throw up or pass out or do something else really awful.

But what if there's a company checker on here? Not giving a welcome-aboard announcement at a major terminal is a Master Operator mark-down. This was no time for something like that.

He was due to get his Master Operator badge in four weeks, and he had already imagined with Kodak clarity what it would look like on the front of his uniform cap, how passengers and other people would react when they saw it up there. He was great at imagining things before they happened. It was one of the reasons he was such a good bus driver, because it helped him anticipate traffic, weather and other hazards of the road in time to avoid tragedies and other problems.

"Good afternoon, folks," he said. The words came out cleanly and that stopped the nausea. He had always liked his voice; he thought it had a nice deep Master Operator kind of tone to it. He hoped it sounded that way to her.

She was still looking out of the window, not at him.

His leg stopped shaking.

"Our travel time to Corpus Christi this afternoon will be two hours and five minutes. My name is Jack. Jack Oliver. Jack *T.* Oliver. If I can assist you in any way or do anything to make your trip more comfortable, please give me a holler. We are glad you have chosen to ride with us today on Great Western Trailways. We call ourselves The Easiest Travel on Earth and that's what we are. Thanks. Now let's hit the road for Corpus, the Valley and points south."

He gave a smart salute to the bill of his uniform cap, performed a half-military about-face and lunged in two strides into the driver's seat. He gunned the motor, released with his left hand the emergency brake lever that came up from the floor on the left side of his seat, double-clutched and with his right hand put the bus in first gear by gently shoving the round black knob of the from-the-floor stick shift forward and to the left.

Safety regulations required that he look into the inside rearview mirror to make sure all passengers were seated before leaving a terminal. Unless there were standees, which there were not today. Only twenty-six of the forty-one passenger seats were occupied.

She moved her head to the front, toward him. He caught her eyes. Was that a smile? Did she smile at me?

Yes, I think she did. She did. I swear she did.

He let out the clutch, eased the bus up to the sidewalk at the edge of the driveway, made sure no pedestrians or cars were coming and turned the steering wheel steadily and powerfully to the left. The bus glided onto the street, Main Street. It was a maneuver he had made hundreds of times but this time he felt a special sense of power and accomplishment, as if his extraordinary skills were on display on a stage. That was because of her. He wondered if she was watching him now. Did she see how he handled this big machine?

He peeked up into the mirror. She was looking out the window again. But he had the feeling she did so just then, just a whiff of a second before he looked at her. She did not want him to know she was watching him.

He was sure of it.

He had to make another left turn in two blocks at Commercial Street to head back to the west to Moody Street, which was U.S. Highway 59-77 through town. This time he would try to keep a good eye on her.

Now that was really stupid, Jack. Why in the world would a beautiful, sophisticated woman like this, a White Widow, want to watch a simple, dumb bus driver make a simple, dumb turn to the left?

But maybe she does realize how hard it is to turn one of these wheels, particularly this one. Bus #4101 had always had a stiff steering mechanism. He had written it up on the Trip Report several times, but it was still there. The easiest turner was #4207, which he often drove the other way, coming northeast out of Corpus.

There was no way to account for the differences in buses. They could come out of the same factory one right after the other and be completely different to handle, not only in the way they steered but in their braking, pickup, steadiness on the road and several other things. On the steering, they were talking about putting power steering on the new buses, but that was probably still years away. For Great Western, at least. Greyhound already had a few of their new Supercoaches with air-assisted power steering on them. Turning one of these Great Western ACF-Brills required perfect coordination between speed and power. He knew several guys who never made it out of probation onto the extra board because they simply could not get the hang of it. They had to give up on being an intercity bus driver.

She must know this. She must know she is in the hands of somebody special, somebody who is also trim and firm and sharp and polished in his uniform.

Oh, don't be stupid, Jack T. Oliver. Even if you're not fat anymore, you're still only a bus driver. Nobody but their mothers and wives and little boys see bus drivers as anybody special.

But she had smiled. He was sure she had smiled.

It Happened One Night came back to him like it was showing on a large screen with full sound right there in front of him. It was a movie he saw when he was a kid that made him realize for the first time that there was a lot more to buses than he thought. Claudette Colbert, an heiress on the outs with her rich father, ran away on a Greyhound bus. She met up with Clark Gable, a newspaper reporter who had just been fired, and love bloomed, despite their very different backgrounds and stations in life. That was all great, but what also caught Jack's attention was the way the bus driver, played by Ward Bond, tells Gable to shape up or get a sock in the nose.

The light was green at the intersection at Main and Commercial and there was no oncoming traffic. But a black Ford had stopped and was now waiting at the red light to cross on Commercial from the west, to Jack's left. This meant Jack had to judge the turning distance exactly right or he would either take off the front of the Ford or run the right front tires of the bus over the curb on the far right side.

Watch this, White Widow! What is your name? You know mine now. I told you, along with the others, just a minute ago. Were you listening? I am Jack T. Oliver. Who are *you*?

Claudette Colbert? Nope. You know who you look like? Ava Gardner. That's what I'll call you. Ava.

Hi, Ava. Are you watching me?

He waited a beat too long before whipping the steering wheel all the way to the left. The bus missed the car but the right front tire scraped against the curb. It was only a slight brushing. Only a small mark would be left on the tire. There was no danger, no problem. It would not even have to be reported.

Did Ava notice? Once he had come out of the turn and straightened out the bus he looked in the mirror back at her. She was gazing out the window.

He shot his eyes around to the other passengers sitting behind. Did any of them see or feel what happened?

Nobody seemed to. Nobody looked scared or worried or upset or annoyed. Everybody looked perfectly happy to be on #4101, Great Western Trailways' 3:15 P.M. bus from Victoria to Corpus Christi, a Silversides Thruliner, from Houston to Brownsville in the Rio Grande Valley.

But, my God, let this be a lesson, Jack T. Oliver. You would never have scraped that tire if you hadn't been thinking about that beautiful woman, that Ava. Never. A good lesson. Master Operators do not allow anything to distract them, Jack T. Oliver. Particularly beautiful women.

But this was more than just a beautiful woman. Oh, so very, very much, much more. More. She really was a White Widow, the bus driver's ultimate dream woman.

Are you watching me drive this bus, White Widow Ava?

He made another left turn onto Moody Street with no problem and then he was on the highway. Five blocks of houses later he was across the Guadalupe River Bridge, past the Circle Bar 12 Paradise Motel, the Conoco station and Fred and Larry's Automotive Service out on the open road.

In a few minutes and miles U.S. Highways 59 and 77 parted, 59 running straight west through Goliad, Beeville, Mathis and Alice to Laredo. Highway 77 turned south toward Corpus Christi.

Jack made the turn with 77. He whistled some air out of his mouth and shook his shoulders slightly. Here he was again, out on the road at full speed. On the open road at full speed. Again, again, after each stop in each town, it happened to him day after day, run after run. No other experiences in his life electrified him, aroused him, thrilled him the same way.

He eased the speed up to fifty and then to fifty-five. Greyhound had their GMC Supercoaches and all of the fancy rest, but nothing was as good as an ACF-Brill. The Hall-Scott engine pancaked in the middle of the bus gave it stability and heft in the center. The GMCs were pushers, with their motors in the back. It made them slower on hills and wobbly in crosswinds. No bus held the road like an ACF-Brill.

The bus felt good, sounded good. He could feel the soft, slight, solid vibration of the Hall-Scott engine in the steering wheel. Already more than six years out of the ACF-Brill factory in Philadelphia, #4101, according to the driver's Trouble Log, showed only minor problems, in addition to its stiff steering. A windshield wiper had gone off the track, two inside lights had shorted out, the air conditioning had been slow to kick in twice, an inside dual tire on the left rear had been blown by a nail. Nothing serious. It was a fine piece of equipment and it made Jack feel good to be its driver, its captain.

The White Widow, his Ava, was still looking out the window. Or were her eyes closed? It was hard to tell for sure.

Look this way! Look at me!

Jack cut his eyes from the outside rearview mirror on the left to the one on the right. Back and forth, ever so slowly every five to six seconds. A surprised driver is a reckless and dangerous driver, they said in operator school. Any driver who does not know at all times if there is a car or a truck or a tractor or a dog or any other moving object behind him or alongside him is an unsafe driver, an amateur. It is impossible to react correctly to an emergency if you have to first see what's going on around you. The second or two that can take can be enough to make it impossible to react to a blowout, to a car turning out unexpectedly in front of you, to a patch of ice.

All of that was automatic to Jack now. Even when he was driving his own Dodge to the corner to pick up something at the store he did it, he moved his eyes from one side to the other in a five-second rhythm.

Her magnificent head was still facing outward, to her left. There was nothing to see out there. Nothing of consequence. Just flat land of what they called the coastal bend, some patches of good black land but mostly scrub grass and sandy light-brown dirt and shallow gulleys and white gravel roads.

What are you looking at, Ava dear?

The route ran parallel to the coastline about thirty miles inland all of the way from Houston down to Corpus. It was a distance of 287 miles. The Great Western Trailways schedulers allowed five hours and fifteen minutes to make it. There were some drivers who could never make it on time. There was something in their makeup, something in their personality, in their very being, that simply made it impossible for them to move their buses and their passengers down the highway and in and out of the terminals and stops in the time the official timetable said they should be able to. Sometimes it was the package express that they had to unload in the small towns. Sometimes it was a late connection in Houston or heavy traffic somewhere. Sometimes, somewhere. They always had a reason, an excuse for running late.

There were others who always ran "hot." Early. Joe "Rocket" Ridgley was the worst. His weird personality made him cut everything as thin and quick and frantic as he could to shave time off the schedule. Everybody said that Rocket had better be careful. It wasn't healthy to be that frantic about anything. It could kill him in more ways than one. It could kill him with high blood pressure or ulcers or something like that, or, some of the drivers said, it could also kill him right out there on the highway. It was well known that Rocket got impatient to pass and sometimes took chances in his driving. Everybody said it was a wonder no checker had caught him and canned him because of it.

Jack believed that a schedule was a schedule. You weren't supposed to be hot or late. He was obsessive about it and that was the reason the other drivers and most everyone else called him On Time. Most of the drivers, like major league ballplayers, had nicknames. His was On Time. On Time Jack Oliver. He didn't mind. It was important for him to know that if a bus was due in Refugio—which was pronounced "Reh-fur-ee-oh," not "Reh-foo-gee-oh"—at 4:17 P.M., as this bus was, the people of Refugio, Texas, could look up from whatever they were doing at 4:17 and remark, "Well, well, there's the four-seventeen Great Western to Corpus."

What is she looking at now?

CHAPTER 2

*T*here was Refugio.

The Great Western Trailways commission agent in Refugio was Adele Lyman, an unhappy woman whose real business was supposedly selling real estate and Verdigris Valley Life and Casualty insurance. It was a business she had taken over from her husband, who had died in the line of duty as a volunteer fireman. He was at a house fire when a beam fell on him, knocked him down and crushed his back so he couldn't move and escape the smoke that filled his lungs and killed him.

Jack pulled up #4101 in the marked-off parking area in front of Adele Lyman's place at 4:20.

Four-twenty. Three minutes late! Jack opened the door to the ACF-Brill and climbed down and out. The door was operated by air, just like the brakes. There was a lever on the right-hand-bottom side of the dashboard that triggered the air, a swisssh sound and the opening of the door.

He had left Victoria right on the money. There had been no passengers to discharge or pick up at Inairi or Vidauri. What had happened to make him late? He kept his Gruen wristwatch precisely correct. Every morning before he left his home in Corpus or his hotel room in Houston he called the time-check number.

But he hadn't looked at it since he left Victoria. That was unusual, too. He always routinely checked his watch every few minutes. Like clockwork he checked his watch.

"What have you got for me today?" Jack said to Adele inside the rundown office that doubled as the bus depot.

"Two Tamales and four Dollars, sweetie, and some roses for Billie's Flowers in Woodsboro," she said. Jack could not imagine any citizen of Refugio buying either real estate or insurance from Adele Lyman. He couldn't tell if she was stupid or was drunk all of the time, but the result of whatever bothered her was that her hair, which was light brown, was never combed, and her dresses, which did not fit, were stained with food. She was probably in her late fifties but she looked, sounded and smelled seventy. One of the other drivers said her only problem was that she could not get over the loss of her husband in that house fire. Jack thought that was probably right. Why else would a woman not comb her hair or wash her clothes?

Jack and the other drivers figured it was only a matter of time before a Great Western district passenger agent, a DPA, came through and took the bus depot away from her. The 10 percent commission she got on all bus tickets and package express, like the shipment of roses to Woodsboro, was probably her only income. Too bad, but she was definitely not good for the bus business in Refugio.

When she said "two Tamales" she meant two Mexicans. Two people, two passengers. She called all Mexicans

Tamales. She called all Negroes Blues, all bus drivers sweetie, and all other people, including well-dressed Anglo passengers, Dollars. So her report meant there were six passengers and a box of flowers for the 4:17 to Corpus and points south.

Jack grabbed the brown cardboard box of flowers, which was long, like a small casket, and light, and yelled, "All aboard for Corpus and the Valley!"

Six people got up from a group of half-broken black-vinyl-and-chrome chairs off in one corner and followed him outside. Those chairs were the only things in the place except for a cluttered desk and a matching swivel chair and a wire rack full of Great Western timetables, most of them long out of date.

He helped the people to board, stuck the flowers in the rear outside baggage compartment and hustled back to the door of his bus.

"They're going to fire your butt, Jack," said Adele Lyman. She had followed him outside. "Three whole minutes late. You were three whole frigging minutes late. Naughty, naughty Jack. Naughty, naughty. What has come over On Time Jack Oliver? The checkers will get you if you don't watch out."

Jack waved her words away, got back up and behind the wheel, gunned #4101 and eased her out onto the highway.

It was only after he had her in fourth gear, cruising gear, back on the road and moving at a good solid speed, that he finally took a look at his beautiful lady Ava, his White Widow.

Her head was back on the headrest. Her eyes were closed. Definitely. Her eyes were definitely closed. And she was no longer alone. A Refugio passenger, one of Adele Lyman's Dollars, was now sitting next to her. The Dollar was a middle-aged woman who looked like she was somebody's teacher. The beautiful lady was perfectly safe.

How old is she? Older than thirty? Jack had not gotten that good a look at her close up, but, yes, more than thirty. There was something in that marvelous face and skin that showed that much age. Maybe a little more. She was a woman of some substance, some living. Was she a telephone operator? Or a nurse? No, no. A teacher? Or maybe she was nothing?

Jack saw her handling a long-distance call from him to his grandmother in San Angelo. Then applying a tourniquet to his bleeding right leg. Then putting an algebra problem on a blackboard and calling on him, at age fifteen, to explain to the class what it was all about.

Then he saw her doing nothing but sitting on a stool at a Walgreen's lunch counter, sipping a cup of coffee with cream and sugar, eating ever so gently a piece of lemon meringue pie.

He quickly spun his eyes toward the outside mirror on the left and then slowly to the one on the right. A blue Ford had come up behind him while he was watching the lady. The Ford was impatient to get around him. Jack watched him swing out to the left to check the oncoming traffic and then slide back.

Hey, calm down there, buddy.

A semi was coming from the other direction. There had been talk of widening 77 to four lanes from Victoria all the way to Corpus. But it did not make sense to Jack. The traffic was seldom that heavy, except on holidays and some weekends. But this guy in the Ford, whoever he was and wherever he was going, would probably not agree.

The truck passed, the oncoming lane cleared, and the Ford zipped on around. Jack estimated the guy's speed at seventy-two or seventy-three miles per hour.

Hey, Slick, where are you when we need you? Slick Carlton was the Texas highway patrolman who usually worked this road. They called him Slick because he wore his hair like some movie stars did, combed straight back and sopped with hair tonic. He was stationed in Sinton and lived there, but he was originally from Port Arthur, sixty miles east of Houston, right on the coast south of Beaumont. The joke out on the road was that Slick's mother had been a madam at one of the many whorehouses Port Arthur provided to serve the merchant sailors who came to port in search of fun and favors. Slick always denied it, but halfheartedly and with a laugh.

Jack goosed #4101 up to fifty-nine miles per hour. Fifty-five was the legal limit, fifty-seven was the company limit. But he needed to make up some of that time he had lost, he did not know where. He could not get all three minutes back between now and Woodsboro, just thirty-five miles away, but he could get a minute. Close to it, at least. Then maybe another between Woodsboro and Sinton, before opening it up even more on the four-lane from Odem on into Corpus.

Jack loved the fact that some of the drivers, his admiring friends, talked about a special sense he had of the connection between his speed and his schedule. One guy said it was a lot like the sense Indians have about animals.

He wondered if the beautiful lady snored when she slept. Loretta did when she slept on her back. Loretta was his wife.

He saw the woman, Ava, asleep on her back on a big four-poster bed. Her beautiful blue eyes were closed, her beautiful dark hair fell like a queen's crown around her head. She was not snoring.

Hey, Ava, open your eyes and let me take a good look at you!

He glanced down at the speedometer. Fifty-three, it said. He had let it slip back down.

The depot in Woodsboro was at the El Hacienda Motor Court right on the highway. The only way anybody would know it was the bus depot was the small red, cream and blue porcelain sign that hung on a bracket out front. It was oval, about two feet long, with the words GREAT WESTERN across the top, the picture of an ACF-Brill IC-41 in the center and BUS DEPOT across the bottom. The lettering was in standard Trailways style—called macaroni because the letters resembled pieces of fat macaroni.

Jack stopped the bus with the sound of the air brakes, exactly four minutes late.

Not only had he not made up a minute, he had lost one.

It was that White Widow back there. He simply could not think about her and imagine about her and watch her and drive this bus at the same time.

Okay, Jack T. Oliver, straighten up. Square yourself and your mind away, Jack T. Oliver, On Time Jack Oliver. You have a schedule to keep. You are about to become a Master Operator.

Turn off that big imagination of yours and do your job, On Time Jack Oliver. Your reputation and your whole life depend on it.

—

He lost two more minutes after Woodsboro, pulling his bus into the Union Bus Terminal at Peoples and Schatzel on Lower Broadway in Corpus Christi at 5:56 P.M., exactly six minutes late. He had been late before, because of bad weather, a mechanical failure or a late connection at Houston from Dallas or New Orleans, but not since he was a rookie had he actually lost six minutes on a schedule for no real good reason.

For no real good reason like having a genuine White

Widow sitting in the fifth-row left-side window seat. He had had beautiful women on his buses before. Many of them. Hundreds of them. Some of the drivers, he was convinced, drove buses solely to meet women. They were like ship captains in the movies; they kept girlfriends all along the route from Houston to Corpus, Corpus to McAllen, Houston to Dallas or wherever they drove. But Jack was not one of those. He had never made a pass at a woman passenger, or even a veiled suggestion of such a thing. He saw them and enjoyed the view but that was always as far as it went. Even in his mind.

That is what made this so different, so incredible, so shaking.

And it wasn't because she was *that* beautiful even. He had had a young woman on his bus one time who went on to become Miss Wharton and third runner-up for Miss Texas. Billy Hobby, the agent in Wharton, still talks about her coming in there in tight silver pants and white boots with her mother and buying a one-way to Fort Worth.

No, there was more to this woman in a fifth-row left-side window seat than just being gorgeous, than just looks. But what?

Maybe it was a spiritual thing. Some kind of spirit in her had wrapped itself around one in him. There was nothing that could be done to stop it, or even to slow it down. Like the waves coming in on the beach on Padre.

Maybe "love" was the word for it. Love? Oh, come on, Jack. How can you be in love with a person when you do not even know her name and the only words you have exchanged are:

"All the way to Corpus."/"That's right."

"Have a nice trip."/"Thank you."

What was love anyhow? He told Loretta he loved her and

he meant it when he said it. He really did. He meant that he was glad the two of them had met and decided to make a life, have sex and decorate their house at Christmas together.

He and Loretta were famous in their neighborhood and in their entire part of Corpus Christi for the Christmas displays on their house and on the lawn. One year they'd even had a picture of Oscar in the *Corpus Christi Caller,* where Loretta worked as a supervisor in the classified advertising department. Oscar was Loretta and Jack's half-life-size Santa Claus.

He took one last look at the White Widow in the rearview mirror as he set the emergency brake.

Do you decorate your house at Christmas, Ava? Where is your house anyhow?

She was talking to the woman sitting next to her. About what? What exactly did her voice sound like? He had heard her speak so little, it simply was not enough to get a fix. If he heard her speak on the radio or on the telephone or even over a PA system he would not be able to recognize her.

He stood and addressed his passengers for the last time on this run on this day:

"This is Corpus Christi. Those of you going on to the Valley will have twenty-five minutes to eat and do as you like. I will be leaving you here. I certainly do hope all of you have had a nice ride with me this afternoon. By all means come back. We are always going your way, here at Great Western Trailways, to the next town or across America. Please watch your step as you disembark." Jack always enjoyed saying "disembark."

But why did he say all of the rest of that? There was nothing in the company guidelines about saying anything other than warning them to watch their step and announcing the name of the town and the length of the rest stop. Always going your way. To the next town or across America. They were all Great Western company mottos, used even in some of their radio jingles. Some of the drivers complained about the money those radio ads cost, saying the money should go to employee salaries. Jack didn't feel that way. They made him feel proud. He had heard a new one just the other day that was particularly catchy, he thought. It went:

> It's cheaper by far than driving your car,
> To ride a Great Western Trailways bus.

It's cheaper by far than driving your car, dear lady Ava. We're always going your way, Always. To the next town or across America. Always, dear lady Ava.

Greyhound had had a whole song written about it for a World War II movie starring Van Johnson. "Love on a Greyhound Bus" had made it to Number Two on the *Hit Parade* on the radio for several weeks. Jack figured that nobody would ever write a song like that about Trailways. He loved the words in the Greyhound song.

> Bought a ticket the other night,
> The Union Station was lit up bright,
> The crowd was shovin' with all its might,
> But we all settled down for a trip on a Greyhound Bus.

There were words about heading west, stopping for hot dogs and soda pop, cuddling up close to you, asking the driver "How long till we make another stop?," moving on through Columbus, Ohio, Indianapolis, Indiana, and being delayed by a bridge out, a Texas storm and a driver who "mistook Illinois for Iowa." It ended with:

> But we'd be happy in any state,
> 'Cause we both fell in love on a trip on a Greyhound Bus,

That's us.

In love on a Greyhound Bus.

Was that what he, Jack T. Oliver, was now doing? Was he actually falling in love on #4101, his own Great Western Trailways bus? He was in love with Loretta, wasn't he? How could he fall in love with somebody else?

He was in love with Loretta, wasn't he?

One by one the passengers came to the step and let themselves down to the ground. Jack stood at the bottom and took each person by the elbow and assisted him or her. Great Western Trailways, the route of the Silversides Air-Conditioned Thruliners, was not keen on getting sued by people who fell or tripped getting off a bus. A Wichita Falls–Dallas driver was fired two years ago after such an incident. He turned to talk to a porter instead of paying attention to passengers disembarking at the Wichita Falls depot. An elderly man stumbled, fell facedown on the pavement and suffered a concussion.

Jack could feel her coming. The White Widow was approaching.

He tried to glance up to see her but she was still out of sight, still back down the aisle, waiting her turn.

Now, there she was. Those blue eyes were right on him. Then they looked down to see where she was going, to watch her step.

He reached for her elbow. Velvet smooth. Oh, still so ever velvet smooth. And there was a smell. How could he have missed it before? It was perfume. No, a soap. Good, expensive soap. She must have bathed right before catching the bus in Victoria? The idea of her coming directly from a bathtub to #4101, his bus, sent warmth to his face.

"Watch that step now," he said to her. Of course, that was what she was already doing.

She smiled. But not enough to even show her teeth.

He removed his fingers from the velvet. And she walked away toward the terminal door.

"My turn?"

A woman in her sixties, a Dollar, was on her way down the step to the ground.

"Yes, ma'am," he said, turning back to take her elbow.

By the time she was down and he could look back at the terminal door, the White Widow was out of sight.

She had left him without saying even a word of good-bye or regret. Would he ever see her again?

He wished there was a way to capture a smell in his nose and hold it for a while. That soap smell was there now but he knew it would soon be gone. He could imagine the bathtub and her in it, though. Yes, yes. He knew he could do that. He knew he could hold that for the rest of his life.

——

The other drivers gave him a hard time for being late.

"We were about to call the highway patrol, the Coast Guard, the Kiwanis and the Camp Fire Girls," said Jumping Jimmy Dale Hayes, the driver who was waiting to take the schedule on to Brownsville. His nickname came from the fact that he couldn't sit still for long, except when he was driving a bus. "Where, oh where, had our little Jack gone?"

"Calling all cars, calling all cars," said Okie Owens, whose first bus job had been with Missouri, Kansas and Oklahoma Coaches out of Pawhuska, Oklahoma. He spoke through his hands cupped in front of his mouth. He was driving the 6:30 connection straight west out of Corpus to Alice, Freer and Laredo. "Be on a lookout for On Time Oliver and his big ACF. Calling all cars, calling all cars."

There were three other drivers, two from the extra board, in the drivers' room behind the ticket counter. Working off the extra board was how and where everybody began at Great Western. Extra-board drivers spent their days and nights always on standby at depots or by their phones at home, waiting to pull a double or a charter, to drive a scheduled run for a sick or vacationing regular. They got rich over the holidays and in summer and other heavy-traffic periods, but since they were paid only minimum "protection" wages when not actually driving, they could come close to starving the rest of the year, particularly in the travel-business dog days of January, February and March.

Everybody got into the act kidding Jack.

"Six minutes. Six minutes late. A record."

"They ought to never give him that gold badge now."

"What kind of example does that set for the young drivers coming along?"

"If On Time Oliver is late, then what's next?"

"The Japs will win next time."

Jack laughed with them and took it. But he said nothing about what had happened, offered no explanation at all for the lost six minutes. He didn't even make up a good lie about a crazy passenger in Wharton or an overturned tractor trailer outside Louise.

He signed all of the reports and the logs, said good-bye to everyone, took his small black leather suitcase and headed out for home. Loretta would have dinner for him. It was Friday, which usually meant meat loaf, one of his most favorite foods. Loretta had finally learned from his mother how to make it the right way, with chopped green peppers and a little maple syrup in there with the egg, the ketchup, the mustard and the dry Wheaties cereal.

He walked two blocks to the bus stop at Lancaster and Chaparral. There were three Tamales, a Blue and two Dollars waiting for a bus. In less than three minutes there it came. The Alameda–Staples, one of three main lines through Corpus. Jack had driven that run himself many times when he worked for Nueces Transportation Company, the Corpus Christi transit line. That was where he started his career as a bus driver when he was twenty-two years old.

The bus hissed to a stop. It was a GMC TDH-3612 in its blue-and-white Nueces Transportation livery. The *T* was for "transit," the *D* for "diesel" and the *H* meant it had hydraulic automatic drive rather than manual drive. Some of the Great Western drivers longed like whiny babies for the day when automatic drives would come to ACF-Brills and other intercity buses, but Jack did not agree. Double-pumping the clutch while moving the gearshift stick from first, to second, to third and on to fourth was a vital part of being the master of that big machine. Jack couldn't imagine anything more boring than just putting his foot on the accelerator and having the gears shift automatically without his doing a thing, like he wasn't even there.

N.T.C. ran small Ford transits when Jack was working for them, and he hated them. They sounded like rubber bands twirling around in a tin can and they overheated in hot weather, which there was a lot of in Corpus.

"Hey, Jack," said the N.T.C. driver. "You're running late."

"Hey, Floyd," said Jack as he stepped aboard. "Late connection in Houston."

Jack knew all of the Nueces Transportation boys. Usually he caught the 6:30 for the twenty-minute ride out to where he lived. This time it was the 6:40. None of the drivers ever made him pay the fifteen-cent fare. They treated him like he was a postman or a policeman, who, if in uniform, could ride the transit buses of Corpus Christi free of charge. The N.T.C. drivers saw Jack as a distinguished alumnus, one of their own who had gone on to better things as a driver of an inter-city bus.

"Get any in Houston?" Floyd asked.

"Oh, the two usual blondes and a brunette," Jack said.

Floyd Cutlersen, a man in his late thirties with no apparent aspirations to go on to intercity driving, believed all he was told about the life of the over-the-road bus driver. Jack tried never to disappoint him with the truth. Like most every bus driver and most every other man he had ever known, Jack never minded other men thinking he was something with women he was not.

"Which was the best?" Floyd asked.

"The brunette."

"What did she look like?"

"Like Ava Gardner."

"Are you serious? What did she do?"

"She didn't do a thing but just sit there," Jack said.

"Oh, come on, Jack. Tell me every detail."

Every detail, every detail, every detail was running through Jack's mind, again and again, over and over.

The bus came to another downtown stop. Several more passengers got on.

Jack moved to the seat next to the window so somebody could sit down next to him. It was already dark, so there were mostly only lights in store windows to see. But he didn't even see them.

He saw only the White Widow in the fifth-row left-side window seat. He felt the smoothness of her skin on her elbow, smelled the soap on her body, admired the blue of her eyes.

He saw that bite on her right leg. He regretted not getting a second look at it when she left the bus. But there was no opportunity.

He saw her in a white porcelain bathtub that was large and stood up off the floor on four fancy short legs. She was splashing hot foamy water up on her body. He felt warmth in his face and some movement and some sensation lower in his body.

The thought of not seeing her ever again in his life made him hurt. He actually felt a sharp pain right behind each of his eyes.

He smelled the syrup in the meat loaf the second he opened the door. It was one of those things that connected his present life in Corpus and on the road to all of the early part back in Beeville. Daisy Lee, the Blue maid, made meat loaf that way when he was growing up, and his wife made it that way now that he was grown.

"It's me!" he yelled once inside.

"You're late!" she yelled from somewhere in the back of the house, he assumed the kitchen.

"Had a lot of package express to write up!"

And there she was. Her short dark brown hair was combed and her cotton dress, a green one with tiny white flowers on it, was clean and starched and pressed. It covered everything but her thick bare arms.

Loretta had weighed 147 pounds when Jack went from Nueces Transportation to Great Western. She still weighed about that. He had gone from 225 to 167 in that same fifteen years because he had to to keep his job after the war, when the veterans came back to work. The company was willing to make exceptions to its weight rules to get drivers during the war but not afterward. Mr. Glisan, the district superintendent in Houston, told him straight: "Slim down or it's back down to transit, Jack." Nobody said anything like that to Loretta at the *Corpus Christi Caller* classified advertising department, so she did nothing serious about her weight problem. As she said more than once to Jack, "If God had wanted me to be tall and skinny, that's what I'd be." It was only a few times more than once that she said it because after Jack got way down they no longer talked about it, continuing to act like they were still the overweight lovers they had begun as.

"On Time Jack Oliver returns again," she said, reaching for him.

"On Time Jack Oliver always returns again," he said.

It was one of their standard greetings, one of what they called their love jokes.

They threw their arms around each other and kissed hard on the mouth. It was what they always did when he came in after a night away in Houston.

Jack patted her on her rear end and they moved toward the kitchen together. His eye fell to her legs. There was no bump on either one of them.

———

He very much wanted to make love. He was used to having that feeling when he returned from an overnight run. It went with being a bus driver. It went with captaining a speeding motor coach full of precious human cargo down the highways and through the cities and towns of America. That was the line a lot of the drivers used, at least. One of them, a guy who drove Houston–Dallas, said it was a scientific thing. His wife, who was an operating-room nurse, said rodeo riders, jockeys, bicycle racers, tractor operators and other men who had their private parts rubbing up against something for long periods of time all had the same sensation and need when their day's work was done.

The terrible part of Jack's feeling tonight was that he could not imagine having sex with Loretta, the only woman he had had it with, not only since they married but in his whole life. She was the first and the only, except in his mind, where he had been very active since junior high school. The only real activity besides Loretta had been some necking with secretaries from the traffic or operating departments a few times after company safety parties in Houston. It had always made Jack feel bad and guilty and ashamed when he remembered what he had done, and he always vowed that it would never ever happen again.

But that made him very, very unlike so many of the men he drove with. "What would you think about your wife doing what you're doing?" he once asked Ray "Smooth" Jefferson, a Houston–San Antonio driver who was notorious for poking any woman who would let him. "I'd kill her," said Smooth.

There was that additional truth about Jack's not fooling around. Before he put on the uniform of a Great Western driver and began to trim down his weight, there were few opportunities, few women who made themselves available to him. None, to be even more exact about it. He had grown up pudgy in Beeville, a small town north of Corpus on the San Antonio highway, U.S. 181. And he had stayed pudgy through high school, his year of junior college at Del Mar College in Corpus Christi and into a career driving buses. He had also had a serious pimple problem from the fifth grade on, and it all combined to prevent him from ever having a real date with a girl until he was twenty-two, when he met Loretta's cousin Alice Armstrong, who everybody called the All-American Girl!, after the radio show about Jack Armstrong, the All-American Boy. Alice was a revenue clerk at Nueces Transportation Company. One afternoon a week before Christmas, as he was turning in his report and the change from his fare box, she asked Jack if he was "booked" for that coming Saturday night. He sure wasn't, he said. She said a bunch of the girls there in the office were going to have a casual drop-in Christmas-cheer party and were inviting some of the single drivers and mechanics to come.

"You are single, aren't you Jack?" she asked.

"Yes, ma'am," he replied.

"With some of these guys you can't tell for sure," she said. "But I figured you to be for sure."

For sure. Those words hit home, but he went to the party. He had always been a big fan of Christmas. Loretta, who was already at the *Caller,* was there. She, too, was pudgy—overweight—and a big fan of Christmas. For unspoken but obvious reasons the two of them were drawn together almost immediately. They started talking about their mutual love for Christmas lights and other decorations and then moved on to their respective lives dealing with people who ride city buses and call in classified ads to sell cars and houses. Before long they were giggling, mostly about how much fun it would be to fill a front yard with electric reindeer and Santa Clauses, and Jack called her the next day and asked her to go to the movies the following Friday night. She accepted, and within a few weeks he had taken her to see all of the best-decorated houses and stores and, finally, on a warm January Sunday afternoon, to his favorite spots on the beach at Padre Island. They moved on from talking about Christmas decorations and their jobs to talking about love. And a few weeks after that Jack gave her an engagement ring, which he had bought at Martin's Jewelers for thirty-seven dollars. They set May 2, less than five months away, as their wedding date.

They sat now at their small kitchen table, which was also

their dining table, and ate meat loaf and a baked potato, which she covered with sour cream and butter and he ate with only salt and pepper on it. He drank a Falstaff beer, called Flags by everyone at the Tarpon Inn, a tavern he sometimes went to on days off. It was on the bay on the east side of the ship channel.

"Where was all of the express going?" Loretta asked him.

"The what?"

"The express, the stuff that made you late."

"Oh, that. That. It was mostly auto parts to Victoria. Some to El Campo. And some flowers to Woodsboro."

He chewed and swallowed and sipped slowly and silently. And he knew it was only a matter of time before she asked him the question she always asked him at times like this.

"Are you all right, Jack?"

Somebody had told them both that it was part of a joke routine on the stage in England, or somewhere overseas.

"I'm swell, Loretta," he replied, as he always did.

"You seem like something's on your mind besides that meat loaf and me."

"I'm swell, Loretta."

"I hear you, Jack."

"I hear you" was another of their favorite expressions. He brought it home one day from a ticket agent in Houston and she picked it up and now used it too.

She shrugged and told him what she had been doing while he was away driving his Silversides Air-Conditioned Thruliner to Houston and back.

"Kress's had a special on the little blinking red lights so I picked up two dozen," she said. "I figured they'd fit down the sides of the front door if we want them there."

"Good idea. I have thought for a while we needed something there."

Decorating the outside of their house for Christmas was the major project in their lives together. They discussed all year the putting up of lots of lights and stars and Santas and angels and mangers in their small front yard and across the front of their small house. Doing all of that was what first drew them together and it was now important in keeping them together. Jack's interest in decorating for Christmas had begun back in Beeville, where, because of his plumpness, he was asked a lot in high school and around town to dress up as Santa Claus for Christmas parties. He also did it twice for the N.T.C. folks.

"I really am tired of Oscar," she said. "He's worn out and he looks it."

"I love him," he said. "He was our first, you know." Oscar was the name they gave to their four-foot-tall plastic Santa.

"I know."

"I'm still worried about those old green lights we put up over the garage," he said. "That cord is cracking and exposed and it's going to cause a short if we're not careful."

"We're careful, Jack, don't worry."

"But it's dangerous. They could start a fire."

Loretta was now the supervisor of all classified advertising telephone girls. There were twelve of them on a full-time basis, up to twenty at special holiday times, when the calls really poured in.

"Somebody, a man who talked like a Mexican, wanted to advertise for a Social Security card," she said, turning to a report on her work. "He wanted to buy a Social Security card."

"Why?"

"Come on, Jack. You know why. So he could get into the hospital and welfare and everything like that."

"Sure, I get it."

"Well, I'm glad. It looks like they're going to promote Mr.

Starr to San Antonio. I am really going to hate that. He's the only one on the second floor who understands what it's like for our girls to hang on that phone all day with people trying to cheat on the number of words and things like that."

She had complained before about the cheats. People who called in an ad and then didn't want to pay the same per-word price for an "a" or an "and" as they did for something in three or four syllables.

"Little Martha McMullen is going to have a baby. That will be the end of her for us. I really do hate that. Nobody knows boats and marine gear like she does. She grew up over at Aransas around boats and things. Her daddy's a shrimper, so's her brother. I'm hoping to have her train somebody up to full speed before she actually has to go. We've got some time because the baby's not due for seven months. I can hide her in the back for a while, but once she shows she's got to go. The paper doesn't like having pregnant women sitting around where people can see them. Guess they think it'll give people ideas. At any rate, I'm thinking about putting Ann Marie in there. I think she's ready. Her voice is about as sweet over the phone as anybody's we've ever had. She could sell a classified ad to Baby Jesus."

"Baby Jesus?"

"You know, the one in the Bible and the one we put in the front yard."

"Oh, *that* one."

"Did I get your attention finally?"

"Why would Baby Jesus want a classified in the *Corpus Christi Caller*?"

"Anybody and everybody, if they live long enough, will have a need for a classified in the *Caller*. That is our motto." Jack was not the kind of man who thought along funny or witty lines. But the idea of opening up the newspaper some morning and seeing a classified ad in there from Jesus trying to sell off an old Whirlpool refrigerator or Chevy coupe set him off laughing.

"You are something, Loretta Oliver," he said.

"Thank you, Jack T. Oliver. Is that a proposal for something besides apple pie for dessert tonight?"

"You hear me right," Jack said.

———

He went on back to the bedroom while Loretta cleaned up after supper. That was how they always did it. He came into the house, they went right into the kitchen and ate dinner and then he went upstairs and took off his uniform. Loretta liked to sit across the table from him in the gray and black of Great Western Trailways. Jack noticed that her admiration of him in his uniform had increased as he slimmed down.

He had always been a uniform man himself. Beeville, his hometown, was also the home of Chase Naval Air Station, which was a sister base to the larger one at Corpus Christi. Most Navy and Marine pilots went to one or the other, or both, for advanced fighter training after graduating from flight school at Pensacola, Florida. Jack went to the base on special days with his dad and saw a lot of sailors and Marines on the streets in Beeville. "Chase Sets the Pace" was the base slogan. His first boyish dreams were all about flying Navy fighter planes, but that was never really in the cards. First, it was the simple fact that he was really not that interested in going to college, and, second, it was the more complicated fact of his weight. He was driving for Nueces Transportation when the war started and he thought again about the Navy. Then he got his draft notice and eventually was classified 4-F, so that ended that, too.

It was the 4-F that really changed his life. He remembered Ward Bond in *It Happened One Night* and he went to see Great Western, which he had heard was desperate for drivers because so many were going into the service. He went on to lose fifty pounds, as required, and now here he was, about to become a Master Operator. And that, as his driver friend "Progress" Paul Madison would say, was progress, you see.

Jack had learned how to care for a uniform. He hadn't paid that much attention to his gray poplin uniform shirts when he was with N.T.C. Now he had the laundry give them precisely measured military creases down from the shoulder through both pockets. He put wire collar stays in his shirt collars. His gray gabardine trousers and coat were always well pressed and clean. He tied his black tie in a precise military knot and he kept his black shoes shined like they were glass.

The thinner he got, the harder he worked at his appearance. But at the same time it was so much easier to look good in a uniform when you weren't fat. Just being able for the first time in life to wear his pants right across the center of his now flat stomach rather than just below or above the balloon that had been there for so long made a huge difference. He hadn't taken a really good look at himself in a mirror until he was twenty-seven years old.

Their frame house on Cunningham Street was small. They had bought it for $9,075, 80 percent of that handled by a mortgage from the Nueces Savings and Loan Association. The house had two bedrooms and a living room, plus a bathroom and the kitchen. The walls were thin. As he carefully removed his shoes and socks and his tie and his shirt and his trousers, he could hear Loretta rinse and dry and put away every dish, every glass, every knife, fork and spoon they had used at dinner.

Soon she would be finished. Soon she would be in the bedroom.

Now he was, as usual on evenings when they made love, down to his undershorts. He was also down to figuring out how he was going to work himself up to wanting to do it.

And there, like Refugio, she was.

—

The lights were out. Frank Sinatra was singing "Something's Gotta Give" on the record player. There were five songs on each side of the 45.

"Are you sure you're up to this, Jack?" Loretta whispered. It was another one of their jokes.

"I'm sure," he said.

They were in their bed, they were kissing hard and his hands were caressing her body. She smelled of a perfume with a French name she had bought for herself last year. Her lips were large and moist. How she felt to his touch was all he knew of how a woman's body feels. It was the sensation of touching something soft and smooth and loose.

Then in the darkness of that room and of his mind came the face of that White Widow in the fifth-row left-side window seat.

The lips against his got smaller and tighter. The skin under his hands got silkier and tighter.

His nostrils suddenly were filled with the fragrance of an expensive bath soap, as if she had just stepped out of a white porcelain bathtub with legs on all four corners . . .

—

"You are definitely all right, Jack," Loretta said when they were finished. "I don't think you have ever been more all right, Jack, Jack."

He got out of bed to clean himself up. He went to the bathroom.

He could not remember ever feeling better or worse. He was not sure he could ever do this again. He was not sure he could ever again make love to Ava with Loretta.

It wasn't fair to either of them.

He got a cup of coffee in the depot café, kidded around with the waitress and the cashier, and then went back through the terminal to the drivers' ready room. It was 7:45 A.M. Sunday. He had thirty minutes before his run to Houston, a continuation of a through bus from McAllen, would be getting a first call.

She was not in the waiting room. It was ridiculous to think she would be there. She had had a one-way ticket. Even if she did go back to Victoria, it would have been a dream kind of coincidence if she had been there to take Jack's next schedule back. Great Western Trailways ran six schedules a day, every day, from Corpus to Victoria. There had been eight chances for her to go back to Victoria since she came down with him on Friday. She might have returned on the very next one, even.

Baggage. Did she have any baggage on Friday? No, she did not. So that meant for sure she was already back in Victoria.

If that was where she was going. Of course, she could have stayed right there in Corpus. Maybe she was returning from a quick trip to Victoria. Yes, yes, that was probably it. She lived in Corpus.

Where exactly? And how? And with whom? Would she recognize him if they accidentally ran into each other at the Piggly Wiggly or at the movies? Would she know him in civilian clothes?

Uniforms really do change people. And in more ways than just how they look.

He was pleasant and professional to each of the eighteen passengers who boarded his bus. But when he took each ticket, each elbow, when he smiled each smile, he had half an eye back toward the depot door, up the street and everywhere else, hoping that maybe, just maybe, she would come.

He also had a drunk to contend with. He was a Dollar, a white man, in his thirties, unshaven, smelly and dirty. Jack had twice told him that he could not ride the bus to Woodsboro this morning.

"Sleep it off," he said to the man, "and catch the next schedule." Great Western had a policy against "providing passage to intoxicated persons" but left the enforcement to the drivers. Ticket agents were instructed to sell tickets to anyone who could stand up at a counter with money in his hand. The individual driver would decide if that ticket was going to get the customer anywhere on a bus.

Jack was strict about drunks. Not because of their nuisance and noise but because they might get sick and throw up or they might get filled up and urinate or defecate in their pants. The resulting smell and awfulness from that kind of thing on a closed-up bus full of passengers was devastating.

"Let me on this bus or I'll cut you a new one," said the drunk in one last try. Jack had just been given his last call on the PA system and was now ready to go. The man was standing in front of the bus door.

"Out of my way, buster," said Jack.

"I'll slice you up like a tomato."

"Move."

"I'm going to Woodsboro."

"You ain't going nowhere right now."

Jack stepped toward the man. He saw the man's right hand go into his pants pocket. There was the flash of a knife blade. Jack grabbed the man's wrist with his right hand, twisted it around his back and slammed the man face-first against the bus. The knife fell to the concrete and the man shouted, "Jesus!"

Jack shouted at James Birney, the porter, who was at the rear of the bus loading in some last-minute express, "Call a cop."

The Corpus Christi police station was only three blocks away, over on Chaparral. In a couple of minutes a squad car with two officers was there.

Two minutes after that Jack had his ACF-Brill IC-41, #4110, in gear and was easing her out of the depot onto Lower Broadway toward Victoria and Houston. He had a schedule to keep.

At the first red light he glanced in the inside rearview mirror. The fifth-row, left-side window seat was empty. He hated it that Ava had not been there to see what he had done this morning, to see him at his best.

Oh, how brave you are, Jack dearest, she would have said.

All in a day's work, my sweet, he would have replied.

He felt that aching in his body again. He could hardly wait until he got out of the city traffic, again onto the highway, the open road, so he could think about her.

Jack saw Paul M. Madison, known and loved by Jack and others by his nickname, Progress, as one of the many pleasures of going to work each day for Great Western Trailways. Progress Paul Madison. Paul was in the first group of drivers to make Master Operator officially, and he was one in every way that could be defined unofficially as well. He was number three on the seniority roster of all 367 Great Western Trailways drivers, having started in 1934 as a driver for South Texas Coaches, one of Great Western's many early predecessors. His first run was San Antonio to Victoria, and it had been his ever since. Five days a week for more than twenty years he had driven that 234 miles down U.S. Highway 287 in the morning to Victoria and had driven back that evening to San Antonio. When he started, the buses were motor-out-front models and the roads were mostly gravel and mud. Now the bus he drove was a twenty-nine-passenger Flxible Clipper with a Buick pusher engine in the back, and the highway was a solid two lanes of concrete or blacktop. He was known by all kinds and ages of people in the little towns along the route—Nursey, Thomaston, Cuero, Westhoff, Smiley, Nixon, Pandora, Stockdale, Sutherland Springs and Lavernia. The standard story was that Paul M. Madison had looked at more snapshots of children and grandchildren, received more fruitcakes and chocolate chip cookies from little old ladies, more cigars from new fathers, and more proposals of marriage and love from young women than any other driver in the entire Great Western Trailways system. When the company started its "Courtesy Great of the Month" program several years ago, Paul was the first employee chosen. The story in the company magazine, *The Thruliner,* said Paul Madison "stands for treating our customers with the courtesy and respect they deserve and he lives it and demonstrates it every workday behind the wheel of a Great Western motor coach."

He was as important to Jack as he was to any passenger. Jack adored him for setting a terrific example for him and all the other drivers, but it was the delightful man's company that he really treasured. Jack just loved being with Paul Madison.

"Well, On Time Jack, how are you?" he said this morning. "Tell me a good dirty Late story."

Paul was the one who had given Jack his nickname, On Time. He was the one who gave most of the drivers their nicknames: Ice Cream Jackson because he ate little else but ice cream, Snake Eyes Streetman because he had a pair, Haircut Taylor because he always needed one, College Tony Mullett because he acted and talked like he was smart and superior.

Paul got his own nickname, Progress, because of an expression he used a lot. "That's progress, you see" was what he said to sum up most everything that came from company officials in Dallas and most everything he read in the newspapers or heard somewhere, most of which made no sense.

Jack had no good dirty Late stories except the one about the drunk back in Corpus and he did not want to tell that one. So he only smiled at Paul, who was short and squat. His gray uniform shirt and darker gray gabardine trousers were not quite as well pressed and sharp as Jack's. They used to be, but Paul had let himself go a bit in recent years. "All that dude stuff is for you main-line dandies," he had said. "That's progress, you see."

They were at a table in the Victoria depot's coffee shop, the one reserved for Operators Only, back off in a corner. Paul had driven his schedule in from San Antonio. Jack, who had not made up the time lost by the scrape with the drunk, arrived in Victoria six minutes late, but he was now on a

Hold-for-Connection order from the Houston dispatcher. The connecting schedule from Beeville, Alice and Laredo had blown a tire the other side of Goliad. It was being changed, and Jack was told to hold for about fifteen minutes because there were six passengers going on to Houston.

It meant he and Progress Paul would have some time to talk. Unfortunately, Sunshine Ashley, a strange man who drove the Port Lavaca turnaround, was also unloading his bus out on the loading dock. He would be joining them there at the table in a few minutes. Progress had given him the name Sunshine because there wasn't any in his life. Or at least, from the forlorn grimace that was always on his face, there didn't appear to be any.

Jack wanted very much to tell Progress about the woman on his bus Friday. He wanted very much to tell somebody about her, about it, about what it was doing to him.

"Have you ever had a thing with a woman passenger?" Jack asked Paul within seconds after he sat down. He felt some warmth in his face as the words came out. He was sure Paul saw it. Paul did not miss a thing.

"It's none of your business, it's against the rules and the answer is no. Not since I got married, which was twenty-seven years ago. The real answer is, Don't do it, Jack, even if she's a White Widow."

Jack wasn't sure where the expression "White Widow" came from but he had heard it from his first day with Great Western. It meant any mysterious, beautiful, perfect woman passenger who was probably not available. A black widow only better.

"She's a real White Widow," Jack said. "She really is."

"There is no such thing, Jack. It's all up here," Progress said, putting his right hand to his head. "And down here," he said, putting his left hand down on his groin.

"The checkers got a guy on Amarillo–Wichita Falls last week. He had a White Widow, some Presbyterian preacher's wife, who was meeting him during the rest stop at Childress. They were going off and getting more than a rest. Let that be a lesson to you."

"What's the lesson?"

"If you're going to do it, don't do it with a Presbyterian preacher's wife."

"Why not?"

"Because, young Mr. Oliver, they don't know all of the positions."

Jack laughed. "How in the hell do you know that?"

"I'm a reader."

"Where is that written down?"

Paul M. Madison raised the heavy white china cup of coffee to his mouth with both hands. He took a long sip and said, "Only Master Operators know where things like that are written down, young Mr. Oliver. You will soon be a Master Operator yourself and you can see for yourself. That's progress, you see."

Paul took a gulp of coffee and said, "Okay, Jack, what's up? You got the hots for some lady on your bus?"

"Not exactly."

"What does that mean?"

"I don't know."

"Go to dirty movies instead, Jack."

"She's a real White Widow, Paul. I have never seen anything like her. Even in the movies."

"Did you put her in the Angel Seat?"

"Not yet."

"Angel Seat" was what the drivers called a pair of seats on the ACF-Brill directly across the aisle from the driver's seat. Few other makes of buses had them, because their doors opened right up to the driver's seat and all the passengers sat behind him. Some ACF-Brill drivers devoted much energy and charm to steering pretty women into that special seat and to keeping all others—particularly old people who wanted to talk—out of them.

Jack decided right then to go no further with Progress. He could not talk to him about the woman, about his Ava, about how he had thought of little else in three days, about how it had already caused him to think differently about Loretta and his life with her.

He wondered if he could ever talk to anyone about her.

"The checkers got two other guys in the Amarillo Division for taking cash fares," Paul said. "They took movies of it."

"Dirty movies?"

"Nope. Real ones. Somebody stood off in the bushes and shot pictures of the people getting on the bus and somebody else waited at the town where they were going, Vernon, I think it was, and shot 'em coming off. That way there was no question what happened, that the driver stole their money. That's progress, you see."

Sunshine Ashley joined them, bringing no sunshine and a cup of coffee that was almost white because it was more than half milk and sugar. He was a tall, thin, droopy man. "What are you talking about?" he said. "Something awful, I'll bet."

"That's right," said Progress. "White Widows and checkers."

Sunshine's face got even paler and sadder. "What checkers?"

"They're everywhere," Paul said.

"Even down here?" Sunshine said.

"I'm sure they are," said Paul. "We're due for another go."

Sunshine closed his eyes. Jack thought for a second he might have been praying but then figured he had probably never prayed in his life.

It had been at least two years since the checkers came in a

big way to the South Texas Division. Five drivers were fired then for stealing, letting friends and women ride for nothing and other rules infractions.

"They'll get us all before they're through," said Sunshine. It was a typical Sunshine thing to say.

They heard the arrival of the connecting bus from Laredo.

"See you next time, On Time."

"You bet, Progress."

"You probably won't be seeing me," Sunshine said. "They're going to get me."

Sunshine got up and left. "If I ever get like that, have somebody shoot me," Paul said to Jack.

"Will do," Jack said.

Paul said, "Women have ruined more of us than all of the cash fare stealing, bourbon and Cokes and slick highways put together, young Mr. Oliver. Don't do it, Jack. Whatever it is you are thinking about, don't. I am telling you, there is no such thing as a White Widow that's worth losing your job and your life for."

"I hear you, sir."

They toasted each other with their coffee cups and stood up. Jack walked quickly ahead into the depot to get his last call to Houston.

Mr. Abernathy was there at the ticket counter with his suitcase.

"Where you headed today, Mr. Abernathy?" Jack asked.

"I'm going on your bus, sir," said Mr. Abernathy.

"Terrific. Where to?"

"Vera Cruz, Mexico."

"I'm headed the other way, to Houston today, Mr. Abernathy."

"Oh, my, well, that is too bad. Then I will go to Mount Rushmore."

"That's the other way, too."

"Well, well, then maybe another day."

"Why do you want to go to Mount Rushmore, Mr. Abernathy?" It was a question Jack had asked Mr. Abernathy many times before.

"To see Mr. Jefferson." It was an answer Mr. Abernathy had given many times before.

Jack had seen pictures in magazines of the four presidents' heads that had been carved into the side of a mountain somewhere out West. He couldn't remember if it was in Wyoming or Montana or Idaho. Or South Dakota? Thomas Jefferson was one of the four presidents, all right, and he thought George Washington, for sure, was one of the others. And Abraham Lincoln had to be there. But who was the fourth?

He thought about asking Mr. Abernathy that very question right now. But before it could be done, Mr. Abernathy, suitcase in hand, had disappeared through the depot door and headed back to wherever it was he lived between his trips to the bus depot to go nowhere.

Jack wondered again about who this man really was. Johnny Merriweather, among others, thought he might be the Humble Millionaire they were all waiting for. The other favorite fantasy of bus drivers, besides the White Widow, was the Humble Millionaire. In this dream there is a regular passenger, the quiet little old man in the brown workclothes or something who rides to El Campo every other Thursday or something. Upon his death, lo and behold and presto and shazam!, he leaves his favorite Great Western driver or ticket agent or porter a Cadillac, a rice farm, and maybe several million dollars, five oil wells and a dozen beautiful movie starlets.

Jack believed there was no way Mr. Abernathy could be a real Humble Millionaire. Because if he was, he'd be spending his time not getting on airplanes or Pullman cars to Mount Rushmore and other places, not not getting on buses.

Everybody said Mr. Abernathy did not have it all upstairs, and that was probably true. But Jack did not think he was really crazy. He had no trouble understanding why Mr. Abernathy could not get on the bus. Jack didn't think that was crazy. He himself had never been anyplace besides Beeville before he came to Corpus, which was only eighty-four miles away. And he hadn't left Corpus except to go to places close by, like Padre Island, until he went with Great Western. And even then—now—it was mostly just back and forth to Houston.

Going to new places was not easy for anybody.

———

Jack hadn't even really wanted to leave Beeville. He figured he would live there all of his life and die there and be buried there in Mt. Hope Cemetery on the west side of town. He left only because he could not stand to be around his father's disappointment anymore.

His father was Beeville's leading eye doctor, and the first words Jack remembered hearing from him were: "My only ambition is for my son to join me in the practice." Those were pretty much his only words, too. Robert Isaac Oliver, M.D., known around town as Dr. EyeBob, pushed and shoved and kicked Jack into taking math and biology and science classes in school. On Saturdays and in the summer he made him spend mornings at the doctor's office or walking around the Bee County Hospital. From his third birthday and Christmas on, the gifts Jack received were mostly doctor kits and white coats, play stethoscopes and microscopes. Dr. EyeBob never passed up an opportunity to tell anyone about his plans for his son's future, and it became a given. Everyone who knew the Olivers knew that Jack would someday be a doctor and would practice with his father. The father even had a specific eye-doctor job, a "special mission," for his son. As he told Jack: "They're already working on something called a contact lens. There'll be little tiny lenses that will go right on the eyes, replacing eyeglasses. Your special mission will be to learn everything there is to know about them and then to bring that know-how to the people of Beeville."

It could not be. Jack did not want to be a doctor. He had neither the mind nor the desire to learn math or science or to perform the other intellectual tasks required. "I'm not smart enough," he told his mother. He disliked the idea of dealing with people's hurts and ailments, and the thought of fooling with the human eye specifically repulsed him. "It would make me sick every day," he told his mother. Spending his life bringing the know-how about tiny lenses to Beeville was a special turn-off rather than a special mission. "I can't think of anything worse than worrying about those little things," he told his mother. "Anyhow, my fingers are so big, I'm sure I would lose them all the time."

He told his mother but not his father because his mother always said for him not to say anything like that to his father. "I'll talk to him, son," she said each time and every time. Jack was never sure whether she did.

The father and son traveled a torturous, tumultuous road toward a relationship where there was only indifference and silence on both sides. The last leg began when Jack came home with a C-minus average on his report cards in junior high school. Dr. EyeBob got angry at the teachers and the school for not doing their jobs, but he also forced Jack to study for two hours every weeknight and for four hours each Saturday and Sunday. When the bad grades continued in high school, the doctor turned his wrath and frustration completely on Jack, accusing him of not caring, of not working hard enough, of being headed toward failure. It was a wrath that did not turn away until, toward the end of Jack's junior year, it became clear that he was not going to college. From then on the son no longer held any interest for the father.

Jack hung around Beeville after high school, living at a rooming house ten blocks from his parents' big house on Harrison Street, working as a gas jockey at a truck stop on U.S. 81 and eating himself fat. For the next three and a half years he saw his mother and father on holidays and a few other times by accident on the street or in a store. It might have gone on like that forever if his mother had not called him one day at the truck stop and said she had great news and wanted to tell him about it immediately. She came within a few minutes to the truck stop and Jack took her to a back booth in the café for coffee.

His mother, Janet Alexander Oliver, was nineteen years old when she married Bob Oliver. He was a first-year medical student at the University of Texas Medical School in Galveston, and she had been his high school sweetheart in Beeville. She had attended a junior college in San Antonio for two years and then taken a job as a teller in a downtown bank in Beeville. As she told Jack and everyone else, her only real ambition in life had been to be "Mrs. Doctor Bob Oliver." Jack was never quite sure if that was the truth, but it was something he had never talked to his mother about and never would.

"He loves you again, Jack, just like he did when you were little," she said even before the coffee arrived. "He realizes that he treated you unfairly and he wants to apologize and make it better. He knows now that we all have to be what we are, and he can accept you for what you are. He is sure now that he can live with the disappointment because, as he says, that is all a part of life."

She asked Jack to come over for dinner that night for a celebration and to bring his things and move back into his old bedroom. "I'll have Daisy Lee make your favorite meat loaf with the syrup and everything else the way you like it," she said.

They agreed on six o'clock as the time for dinner. But when six o'clock came, Jack was forty miles south of Beeville, sitting in the fourth-row left-side window seat of a Gulf Coast Coaches Aerocoach on the way to Corpus Christi.

At around six-thirty the bus pulled into Sinton. He was now fifty miles away from Beeville. Jack decided that his mother and father had by now figured out that he was not coming to dinner. He closed his eyes and saw his mother go into the kitchen and take the meat loaf out of the oven. He saw his father light a cigarette—he smoked Chesterfields—and slam the stick match hard into an ashtray. He saw the two of them arguing about what might have happened to Jack and what she might have said to him to make him not want to come. He saw her go to the phone and try to find him—first at the truck stop and then at the rooming house. He saw her put the phone down finally and shake her head as she told his father that everybody everywhere said Jack had gone—from his job, from his rented room, from Beeville. He saw him go into the dining room and sit down at his regular place at the dining-room table. He saw her join him a few minutes later. He saw the two of them eat the meat loaf, served with baked potatoes, green beans in butter sauce and cole slaw.

———

All but two of #4203's forty-one seats were taken when Jack pulled into Great Western's Union Bus Depot in Houston at 1:37 P.M. He had made up all but twelve minutes, despite the load, despite the traffic, despite thinking about Ava. A Late Arrival form had to be filled out only for anything over fifteen minutes, so at least he did not have to do that.

Jack hated all of the paperwork. Everybody did. But it was as much a part of the job as air-braking that #4203 with its thirty-nine passengers onboard under the huge loading-dock canopy in Houston. Paul Madison liked to say the first qualification for driving a bus was not a driver's license but the ability to write insignificant information in inaccessible spaces on incomprehensible forms.

Jack completed his trip report and his driver's log and the bus's mechanical log and all the rest after the passengers had disembarked and the porters had unloaded the baggage and express.

The Houston terminal was a joy to anybody who liked buses. There were always ten or twelve buses parked or moving in or out of the five lanes, having just arrived from somewhere or getting ready to go somewhere. There were always lots of people milling about, waiting, eating, drinking, laughing, crying, sleeping. Missouri Pacific Trailways, which ran up to Texarkana as well as to the Valley along the coast route, used the terminal. So did Texas Red Rocket Motorcoaches, which operated to Galveston and Beaumont, and several other small feeder lines. Greyhound had its own terminal six blocks away.

Jack said hello to a few of the drivers and the baggage agent and got permission finally from the dispatcher to take his bus on to the garage. His work on this day was almost over.

He felt a letdown. He always did when he finished a run. The tension built steadily in him from the time he arrived at the depot in Corpus, checked out the bus after it arrived from the Valley, put aboard his first passengers, moved them along the highway and through the towns until he finally reached Houston. As he approached Houston, the bus always got more loaded with people and express, and the highway became crowded with cars and trucks and other hazards. And then suddenly, like rolling off the edge of a table, it was over. *Sssssssssss-ttt* went the brakes and off went the people, the express and all of that tension.

In the early years he looked forward to that final thrill of driving a busload of people into that Houston depot. "Thrill" was the right word, too. It was a little-boy thing, like scoring a touchdown in the Cotton Bowl in Dallas or marching in review as a Navy pilot after getting his wings, two things he had done only in his imagination. Sometimes he imagined there was background music playing, like in the John Wayne movie *The High and the Mighty,* as he made the last right turn off Travis into the terminal, caught the signal from the dispatcher as to lane and position and then eased his coach into place for that final stop, the last *sssssssss-tt.*

He had imagined driving the bus into the Houston depot, with and without music, before he actually did it for the first time, and in the beginning reality measured up to what he had imagined. But then after a while it did not.

Sex with Loretta had run along the same lines. He was certain that would not happen with Ava, his Ava. How could that ever be less than he could imagine?

Do other men have thoughts like this about women all of the time?

There was another part to the letdown of finishing his run in Houston that had nothing to do with all that. It was what always lay ahead for him at night there. Which was mostly boring and nothing much.

Jack could not get used to Houston and he had about decided he probably never could. Houston made no sense. It was where the crazy oil millionaires like Glenn McCarthy spent their money on big cars and new hotels and where the roughest of the seamen came to play while their oil tankers and freighters were loaded and unloaded. The only difference between the millionaires and the seamen was how much money they had. "Rough" was the word for Houston. A man had to be careful going into bars, because Houston people didn't think very long before they decided killing was all somebody was good for. Bang, bang, you are dead, Mr. Bus Driver. The cops were the same way, particularly when it came to Tamales and Blues. In Corpus, people talked before they fought. In Houston, it was just the opposite. At least that was what Jack was told.

Also Houston was too big, and it was growing even bigger, and too fast. Some people said they expected it to be as big as New York someday. That would be the day Jack would have enough seniority to bid a San Antonio or Laredo turnaround and never have to fight his bus's way into Houston anymore. He hoped. They didn't even have any zoning regulations there, like they did in Corpus and everywhere else in the world, so that meant there could be a Conoco station or a Pig Stand drive-in in the middle of somebody's block in Houston. It also had the worst weather of any place in Texas. It was not only hot, which it was everywhere, including Corpus, but it was wet-hot. The humidity was usually up there with the temperature, and just for good measure it liked to rain for a few minutes most afternoons. One of the Dallas drivers who had grown up in northern Iowa said being outside in Houston in the afternoon was like taking a hot shower with your clothes on. Jack agreed.

He always figured the best thing about Houston was its name. Jack, like every other kid in Texas, had had to take a course in Texas history in high school. Not much of it touched him or stuck, except the story of Sam Houston. Sam had come to Texas from Tennessee, whipped the Mexicans at San Jacinto, became the president of the Republic of Texas and then, when Texas went into the union, represented it in Washington as U.S. senator and finally ran it as governor. He was, according to Jack's teacher and books, a rough, smart man who could fight or talk just about anybody out of just about anything. After Loretta and Jack agreed to get married Jack told her if they had a son he wanted to name him Sam Houston.

"But I don't want him called Sam or Sammy, Houston or Houstie, or anything like that," he had said. "I want him called Sam Houston, like it was one name, Samhouston. Samhouston Oliver." Loretta said that would be fine with her. They never discussed it again because they never had a son, or a daughter, and the doctor had said it was unlikely Loretta ever would. Something was not quite right about her reproductive things, he said. She and Jack had talked about someday adopting a child, a boy they could name Samhouston, but it had not happened.

In all fairness to the city named after Sam, Jack had not seen or experienced very much of it firsthand. He had been driving buses in and out of there two or three times a week for twelve years, but what he did when he was there wasn't much and it was almost always the same. He drove into the city from the southwest on Highway 59, which became Main Boulevard. There was a fifteen-block go up the west side of downtown and then across east on Preston to the bus depot, which covered two thirds of a block bounded on the east by Congress, the west by Travis.

He did every arrival day what he did this day. After unloading his passengers and doing his paperwork he drove the bus to the garage seven blocks south on Nagle Street in the middle of a neighborhood of small houses where the Blues lived. Only in Houston could you put a bus garage in somebody's backyard. From there he caught a ride on a bus back to the depot and then walked three blocks to the Ben Milam Hotel. Great Western kept a block of a dozen rooms at the Milam for drivers on layovers. The rooms were small and they weren't fancy but they were clean and just fine with Jack.

A Dixie driver named Livingston fell in with him for the

walk over to the hotel. Dixie was a division of Great Western that went all through East Texas. It had been called Dixie-Sunshine Trailways before being taken over by Great Western. Livingston drove Shreveport–Houston down through Henderson, Nacogdoches and Lufkin. Jack had known him and seen him around for years but they were not good friends. Livingston's first name was Harold but everybody called him by his nickname, which was Horns. Horns Livingston.

"You-all going to stop in with me?" Horns said to Jack as they got to a tavern called the Mirabeau Lamar Bar.

"You know the rules on drinking," said Jack. The layovers were only twelve hours usually, and twelve hours was also the limit on drinking—no driver could have even a sip of alcohol less than twelve hours before pulling a run. The smell of a beer on the breath of a driver reporting for duty was grounds for immediate suspension and eventual dismissal.

"Nah, nah," said Horns, who was from Louisiana and spoke in an accent that Jack thought made his own South Texas one sound like he was from Alaska or somewhere else up north. "The picture show in the next block."

"No, thank you," Jack said.

The picture show in the next block was a theater that showed only girlie movies. Jack had walked by it many times but had never been inside.

"It's not the real thing but it'll do until you can get the real thing," said Horns Livingston.

"Not interested right now, but thanks."

"You-all not interested in women? Is that what you-all not interested in? Are you interested in something else besides women? Is that what you-all are saying?"

"No, that is not what I'm saying."

"You-all a married man, I'm a married man. I don't run around on my old lady, you-all don't run around on your old lady. So what does that leave a man to do? A man who needs to keep himself at a fever pitch at all times, ready to go the second he's back home? What does that leave a man to do, Jack? You-all tell me."

Jack had never met Horns's wife but he had seen lots of photos of her. Horns carried them around with him as religiously as he did his ticket punch and log book. And he seemed to have a new set every couple of weeks. Her name was Janet Lee and she was clearly a well-endowed, well-stacked woman with a lot of blond hair twisted and waved and arranged on the top of her head. The photos showed her behind the wheel of a car, lounging outside on a hammock, smoking a cigarette in a kitchen, picking flowers and doing all kinds of others things.

"I have nothing to say to you about that," Jack said.

"I give Janet Lee everything I have to give, and that means whenever I get home from a run. I mean the second I come through the door, there she stands without a speck of clothes on her body. So I have got to be ready three times a week. Going to these movies helps me stay ready."

It was his talking like this that caused him to get the nickname Horns.

The theater was called the Lone Star Majestic. It may at one time have shown real movies with real movie stars like Ava Gardner and Claudette Colbert and Clark Gable but it hadn't since Jack had been coming to Houston and staying at the Milam just down the street.

Horns gave Jack a wave and headed for the box office. Jack kept walking. He did look at the posters advertising the movie that was showing, *Lovesick Spies Blues*. There were some black-and-white photographs of some of the women who appeared in the movie.

None of them looked a bit like Ava Gardner or even Claudette Colbert.

CHAPTER 5

*T*hen five days later it was Friday again. And there, like Refugio, she was.

She looked exactly the way he had remembered her, exactly the way he had seen her in his mind ever since the previous Friday at this same precise time. The only difference was in the way she was dressed. She had on a purple blouse that had sleeves all the way to her wrists.

It meant he would not be able to feel the touch of her skin again.

"Well, good afternoon," he said as she handed him her ticket.

"Good afternoon," she replied.

Well, good afternoon.

Good afternoon.

He tried to capture the sound of her voice within his head, like on a phonograph record, so he could play it back again. And again.

"One-way to Corpus again," he said, as he read the ticket, punched it and tore it into two parts—one for her, one for him and the Great Western Trailways auditors.

Again, she smiled but said nothing. She took back her portion of the ticket and, with his gentle assistance, stepped up into the bus.

His bus.

He forgot to smell her! He had been so intent on the sound of her voice that he had not smelled her. Had she bathed again in a white porcelain bathtub with legs before catching his bus?

He was actually shaking when he closed the bus door behind her and the eight other passengers who boarded at Victoria. He had trouble getting his ticket punch back into the holster on his right hip. He felt some twitching in his left leg, as if it was about to rattle out of control again, as it had last Friday.

Progress Paul Madison, who had also just had his last call for San Antonio, was there at the counter sorting through his tickets. "Twenty-two peoples, not bad," he said to Jack. "That's progress, you see."

Jack knew Paul would see something in him. Paul never missed a thing.

"You okay, young Mr. Oliver?" said Paul.

"I'm fine, I'm fine." Jack put his tickets in little stacks by towns. "Let's see, three to Corpus, two for Woodsboro, one to Odem . . ."

"Hey, you're shaking," said Paul. "You have a problem with a passenger?"

"No problem. No problem at all."

Jack knew that Paul Madison knew better but he did not press it. "Hasta la vista, boys and girls, one and all," Paul said to Jack and to Johnny Merriweather behind the counter. And he was gone.

In a few seconds Jack heard the smooth revving of the Buick engine in Paul's Flxible Clipper, then the release of its air brakes.

"I have a question, Johnny," Jack said. He could not help himself.

"Sure, Jack."

"There's a woman I just put on. She rode last Friday, too. She looks familiar. Should she? Did she used to work around here or something?"

"You mean the looker?"

Jack felt some warmth in his face. "Yeah, that's the one."

"I wish I was familiar with her. But I ain't. She looks to me like she's got money or something, though. She looks like a White Widow to me."

Money or something. Now Jack hadn't even gotten that far in thinking about her. Money or something.

"Give me a last call," he said to Johnny and turned to go back out to his bus and to her.

Right behind him at the counter stood Mr. Abernathy with his suitcase.

"I'm ready and this time I am really going," he said. Jack had never seen him so direct and happy.

"Get yourself a ticket and let's hightail it," Jack said. "Hey, hey, Mr. Abernathy."

"No, no, I'm not going with you," said Mr. Abernathy, still smiling. "I'm on my way to Mount Rushmore through San Antonio with Mr. Paul Madison and then on west and up."

"Paul just pulled out. That was him leaving as you were coming into the waiting room."

"Oh, my," said Mr. Abernathy. "I will just have to come back."

And again he walked away with his suitcase.

"I feel sorry for him," said Johnny Merriweather. "He's crazy as a red hornet."

"Right," Jack said, never really having heard of red hornets, crazy or otherwise. "Only a crazy person would miss the bus to Mount Rushmore, wherever that is."

"What are you saying, Jack?"

"I don't know what I'm saying," he said. And he really didn't know. "Like I said, give me a last call."

—

She took a different seat. She was on the aisle, on the right, four rows back. He had found her quickly when he made his announcement to the passengers, which he did without losing his lunch or control over his left leg. As Paul would have said, that's progress, you see.

Now he could see her clearly in his rearview mirror. There was a young boy in a clean white T-shirt with SAN ANTONIO YMCA CAMP emblazoned in dark blue on it sitting by her in the window seat. He was a Dollar. Probably in high school. They were talking.

She was a looker all right. Oh my, yes, she was a looker.

She's got money or something. Johnny was probably right about that, too. And she had gone to college. No question she had gone to college. Probably to U.T. at Austin, or that women's college up at Denton. Jack had always rooted for Texas A&M, the Aggies, over U.T., the Longhorns, but if Ava was a U.T. grad he would change his loyalty for her. He would change anything for her. Anything at all.

Jack, as he turned his bus onto Moody Street, suddenly wished for the first time that he could go back and change his life so he had gone on and finished college, even just junior college. For Ava. He wished he had done so for Ava.

But, but, but. If he had done that, then he would probably

have gone on to be something fancier than a bus driver. That would be terrible! He could not even imagine himself as something else. Not since he gave up seeing himself flying fighter planes or scoring touchdowns. He could not imagine a life now anywhere except behind the wheel of an ACF-Brill on the open road.

On the open road at full speed. Again, again, after each stop in each town, it happened to him day after day, run after run.

There were two passengers, an elderly Tamale couple, to let off at Vidauri. There was no bus station there, only a flag stop at a Flying Red Horse Mobil station. He pulled the bus to a stop and helped the couple off.

He smelled something. Something was running hot. It wasn't the radiator. He went around to the side where the air conditioning motor was. Some smoke was coming out of it.

Back inside, back in his seat, he switched off the air conditioning and then stood to address the passengers.

Here I am again, Ava! Look up here at me, please.

"Our air conditioning is not working properly," he said, trying his best to avoid speaking only to her, to Ava. "I have switched it off. This means opening the windows. There are releases and handles there on each. Feel free to open them. If there is a problem, please let me know. It's only about a hundred and ninety-seven degrees outside so it should not be too bad."

There were some laughs. She smiled. Ava smiled. His White Widow smiled at him.

And he was back in his seat, in gear and on down the highway and into his thoughts.

Jack and Ava were in a booth in a nice restaurant, a seafood restaurant along Padre Island Drive that served baked potatoes with sour cream and tiny green chives as well as butter. She was in her light-colored blouse, he was in full uniform.

I cannot go away with you if you stay a bus driver, she said.

I am a bus driver now and forever more, he said, leaning across the table and taking her right elbow in both of his hands. What else could I be?

Start your own shoe store or be a radio announcer? she asked.

I cannot do either, he replied. I have to be out there on the open road, again and again, day after day, where I belong.

Then this must be good-bye, dear Jack.

I cannot live without you, Ava dearest.

You have no choice, Jack dear.

Why can you not love a bus driver?

Because I was brought up to love better than that.

Then it is true you have money or something like that?

It is true.

—

Adele Lyman and four passengers were not the only ones waiting for Jack and his bus in Refugio. So was Slick Carlton, the regular Texas highway patrolman for the area.

"Two wetbacks shook loose from some immigration cops up at Goliad," Slick said to Jack once the bus was stopped. He had his tan uniform Stetson on his head, but Jack could still smell the tonic underneath. Jack also got a whiff of leather from his wide brown belt and holster, from which protruded a very large .38 magnum pistol. "Any candidates aboard your bus?"

Jack was embarrassed to have to say "I don't think so, Slick. But be my guest."

He stepped back up inside his bus with Slick, who had played linebacker for Lamar College in Beaumont and looked it.

Jack, through good habit and practice, normally looked over every passenger he had on his bus. A question like "Any candidates aboard your bus?" would draw an informed answer. But since she, Ava, got on in Victoria, he had been distracted.

Jack watched from the front of the bus as Slick walked down the aisle, silently peering into the faces of the twenty-seven people who were sitting silently watching him do it.

Jack's eyes were on Ava. Hers finally found his.

All in an exciting day's work for a bus driver, he tried to say with his look. It's responsible, difficult, respectable work for a man. Sometimes they turn up wetbacks but sometimes in the process they flush out bank robbers and murderers and rapists.

Rapists?

There was no criminal of any kind on board.

"Somebody told me you were about to get the big gold badge," Slick said.

"You got it right."

"*You* got it right, you mean. I'm ready for something like that."

"When are you due to make corporal?"

"In about a year if one of those damned Indianolas doesn't get me first."

"Indianola" was what a lot of people along this part of the Gulf called hurricanes and most really bad storms. The name came from the town of Indianola, which was right on the water due south of Victoria and Port Lavaca and had been on its way to rivaling Galveston as a major port and railroad center in the late 1800s. But then it was wiped almost off the face of the earth by two killer hurricanes that hit in two Septembers eleven years apart. Hundreds of people were killed and the few big houses that survived were dismantled and moved away to Cuero and other towns farther inland. Cuero, which also called itself the turkey capital of the world, was Progress Paul's hometown. He grew up with the descendants of some of the Indianola survivors.

"Well, I don't have to tell you, we're right into the Indianola season," Jack said to Slick.

"I know, I know, and I can hardly wait to start pulling people out of floating shacks and stranded pickups," Slick said.

They shook hands and in a few minutes Jack was back on his way to Corpus Christi. A good thing about Slick's check was that Jack did not have to say more than a quick "Hi" and "Bye" to Adele.

But he was late. Seven minutes by the time he got to Woodsboro.

And the bus was hot inside. September was mostly as hot as August in South Texas. Jack saw sweat on Ava's face. Sweat on her beautiful face. He so much wanted to help her.

Here now, let me wipe that awfulness from you.

Oh, please, Jack. That would be wonderful, Jack. Thank you oh so much, Jack.

He was sure her sweat did not smell like everyone else's did. He could not imagine anything about her that would smell bad. Nothing, literally nothing at all. Nothing at all.

———

Your hand feels so good there, Ava said.

It feels so good being there, my dear, Jack said.

Johnny Ray was singing "Little White Cloud That Cried" in the background. They were in bed, the lights were out, their clothes were off.

He kissed her gently on the mouth and then around her mouth and on her neck and chest and below.

Oh, my God, Jack, your lips feel so good on me, Ava said.

They feel so good being on you, dearest, Jack said.

He took his time, lingering for full pleasure over each move, each caress, each kiss.

And when it was over, when both had screamed their pleasure to the heavens, they fell back from each other.

"What are they feeding you bus drivers out on the road these days?" Loretta said.

"The same old roast beef, ranch fries and brown gravy," Jack said.

"I think maybe they're spiking it with something," Loretta said. "I have never seen anything like you. Are you ready now for dinner?"

"Yes, ma'am."

"I'll go get it on the table. I hope the meat loaf hasn't burned."

"I'll be right behind you."

She leaned over and kissed him on his naked stomach, turned on the lamp on the table by the side of the bed and got up.

"You called out something besides me just now, Jack," she said. "When you were coming."

"Like what?" he said.

"I couldn't make it out. Ada, Alma, Ava. Something like that. Something with an *A*, or maybe an *R*."

He did not look at her. He kept his eyes on the ceiling. "Sex is making you hear things."

"Well, whatever. It was some fun. See you in a minute."

"In a minute."

He heard her go into the bathroom and he heard her cleaning herself.

Well, whatever. He had walked into the house and instead of going into the kitchen to eat meat loaf, as they did every Friday night, he had said, "Could we go to bed first?"

Loretta said no because the food was ready, but after he took her in his arms and kissed her, she decided a few extra minutes in the oven would not hurt the meat loaf.

There had been no way he could control the order in which passengers got off the bus. He had hoped that maybe Ava would be among the last, so he could say something to her and perhaps prompt her to say something back to him.

Well, well, I trust you had another good ride on my bus, he would say. It's an ACF-Brill IC-41.

I did indeed. I am so fond of the ACF IC-41. What does the IC stand for?

"Inter-city," meaning between cities. "Intra-city" means within the city. Transit buses, in other words.

How wonderfully interesting and fascinating.

I love my work as a bus driver.

I love men who love their work.

Then I don't have to become something else, dear?

I didn't say that, Jack dearest.

There were other imagined conversations he had with her, particularly during the last ten miles on Highway 9 from Odem on into Corpus.

So sorry about the air conditioning, Ava dear.

It's not your fault, Jack dearest, and I barely noticed.

I promise the bus I will be driving next Friday on this run will have an air-conditioning system that works.

Oh, please don't go to any extra trouble just for me.

It is the least I can do for a regular customer.

But this is only my second trip.

Won't there be others?

Oh my, yes. Many others forever more.

And:

I am sorry we arrived eight minutes late, Ava dear.

I was so entertained and pleased by my ride I barely noticed.

I am delighted to hear that. The comfort and enjoyment of my passengers is of great importance to me.

I can tell. You truly enjoy driving this bus, don't you?

More than I can ever express, when you are on it.

I find that admirable. People should enjoy their work or change their work to something they do enjoy.

I am glad to hear you say that. Life's too short is what I say.

That is what I say, too, Jack dearest.

What actually happened was that she seemed to be in a hurry, maybe because the schedule was eight minutes late. At any rate, Jack took her naked left hand to help her down the last step.

"Thank you for riding with us again," Jack said.

"You're welcome," she said and hurried off.

Thank you for riding with us again.

You're welcome.

He kept an eye on her as long as he could. But she disappeared at the end of the bus depot building, turning up Schatzel Street just as she had last Friday night.

He wondered how in the world he could wait another whole week before seeing her again, assuming she came again to his bus the next Friday.

By the time he got home to Loretta his imagination had his body and mind in such a state of agony and excitement that he could not help but make love to Ava with Loretta.

CHAPTER 6

*T*he next seven days—six days and fourteen and a half hours to be precise—were miserable ones for Jack T. Oliver.

He had a right front tire blow on him as he rounded a corner a block from the depot in Wharton. Fortunately he was moving less than twenty miles an hour. The big bus, #4207, jerked savagely to the left and for a few seconds was literally out of his control, but he got it stopped before anything was hit, any harm to persons or property was done.

An angry man, who looked half Dollar, half Blue, took a swing at him behind the bus at Edna. He had been on the bus all the way from Houston, but Jack had not paid that much attention to him until the guy discovered his suitcase was not on the bus with him. He said he had checked it through to Edna from Saranac Lake, New York, four days earlier.

"They said it would get here when I did," he said to Jack, who had the baggage compartment door up to prove to the guy there was no bag in there with an Adirondack

Trailways baggage-check number that matched the one he had in his hand.

"Well, it isn't here, I'm sorry," Jack said, reaching up to close the compartment door.

"That's not good enough, you Texas sunavabitch," the man said in an accent that sounded pure Yankee. He was taller but thinner than Jack. He had not shaved for several days, so he looked very tough.

"Watch your language, buster," Jack said.

"Buster, my ass."

The man swung a fist toward Jack's face. Jack saw it coming in time to throw his left hand up to protect himself. In that hand was the foot-long steel key that opened the baggage compartment door. The man's fist crashed against it at full force, causing the guy to scream with pain and grab his hand. Jack declined the agent's offer to call a cop. Just call Houston, Dallas or somewhere and help him find his bag, Jack said. Jack tried to avoid getting passengers arrested, not just because the company didn't think it was too hot for business but also because if there were hearings and trials later, it meant taking days off and other disruptions.

A baby calf, all black except for large white spots around the eyes, ran out in front of his bus between Inairi and Vidauri. Jack saw it, but there was no way to miss it without either swinging out left into oncoming traffic or heading off the road to the shoulder on the right. Neither was an option, and the poor calf was knocked through the air and landed in a bloody, lifeless heap. Jack and a passenger, a high school boy with a crew cut and a Future Farmers of America blue corduroy jacket, pulled the cow's body into the ditch. The high school kid seemed sad and wouldn't look at or say anything to Jack. He obviously thought Jack could have avoided hitting the animal.

"There was no way to miss him without causing an accident," Jack said as they carried the cow. He had the front legs, the kid had the rear ones. "It was him or us."

"Maybe," said the sad boy, who had boarded at Victoria; Jack knew, from his ticket and his FFA jacket, that he was from Freer, a town between Alice and Laredo.

Nuts to you, kid, Jack thought but did not say.

Animals were serious hazards to buses. A Mack's Motor Coaches Fitzjohn had gone out of control north of Woodville, Texas, recently after hitting a mongrel dog. Two passengers were seriously hurt. A Kerrville Bus Company driver had lost a new Beck bus and his own right eye and leg when he plowed into a bull outside Fort Stockton last year. Jack had also heard of a Blue Ridge Lines driver who died after broadsiding a deer somewhere west of Baltimore, Maryland.

So nuts to you, kid. People are more important than animals.

On Wednesday, his day off, he woke up to rain. He looked outside and saw immediately that it was one of those heavy, steady downpours that would last all day. Among the things it would wash away was the day he had planned in the sand at Padre.

He had been very much looking forward to gazing up at that sky the color of Ava's eyes and thinking about her, and about them together.

"What are you going to do today?" Loretta asked before she left for work. Jack was up but still in the light-blue boxer shorts he often slept in when it was hot.

"I don't know," he said. "Maybe I'll get the lambs out and see if they work."

"You've got three months to do that."

The lambs. There were two of them, painted wood, life-size. He had picked them up at a junkyard near Ingleside two weeks before on his day off. He thought they might work with their Christmas manger set.

"Want to go downtown and meet me for lunch?" Loretta asked.

"I doubt it. I'll call if I do."

"You going to hit the Tarpon then."

"Maybe."

She left and Jack got back into bed, hoping he might be able to go back to sleep.

Maybe he could imagine he was lying in the sand at Padre and do all of the same imagining he would have done out there.

He closed his eyes. He couldn't see anything at first, and then he saw that damned dead cow between Inairi and Vidauri, and all he could hear was the rain on the windows and the roof. He reached over to the bed table and turned on the radio. He hated what was on the radio in the daytime—only dumb story programs for women. Didn't the people who ran radio stations realize that there were a lot of bus drivers and other men out there listening to the radio in the daytime too?

The lambs. He got up, dressed in some jeans and an old uniform shirt and went out to the garage to see about the lambs.

He had to step around Oscar, the Santa Claus, to get to them. The Santa, which was old and made of a thin glass-like material, went on one side of the front yard, the manger on the other. Jack had a special affection for Oscar because he was the first big item they had bought together for their front yard.

The lambs came almost to his waist. Their features were lifelike. One had its head down, as if it were eating grass; the other looked straight ahead, as if posing for a photograph. Both needed to be painted. They would be fine.

Decorating their house and yard for Christmas was his only hobby. Some of the other drivers fished and hunted and collected things like old Coke and RC bottles. Some of the others remodeled their own houses or did handyman work for other people on their days off. There was a driver in Amarillo who did people's income tax returns, and there were others who actually ran real businesses on the side, like liquor stores or appliance fix-it places.

Jack didn't have anything like that to do. Besides playing with the Christmas decorating the only other thing was going to Padre Island to rest.

And occasionally he did go to the Tarpon Inn for a few beers, when it was too wet to go to Padre or he just felt like it.

That Wednesday it was too wet and he felt like it.

But even that didn't turn out well. Nobody he cared about or cared to talk to or even to see was there when he arrived. A Rio Grande Coaches driver named Mitchell Johnson was drunk at the bar when he came in. They called him Wax because of his name, Johnson, and because he was greasy, like table wax. He started telling Jack about growing up in St. Charles, Missouri, outside St. Louis and how his father was a brakeman on the Katy Railroad. Jack didn't care a thing about St. Charles, Missouri, or Wax's dad.

The Tarpon Inn's owner was a painted redheaded woman in her sixties. Everybody called her Willow because she was skinny and seemed to always be bitching—weeping—about something: the high cost of electricity, the stupid city, the dumb beer salesmen, the Fritos route man, the awful weather, the idiot sheriff's deputies.

It was the shrimpers she was hating this day.

"They come in here all stinking like their shrimp, acting like they're tough and God. All of them have those wads of money in their pockets but they all ask for credit and then I have to scream and pull every dime out of them. I have had it with them, Jack. Had it. And besides that Eisenhower's a Communist."

Besides that Eisenhower's a Communist? It was the second time Jack had heard that in the last several days. What's going on with Eisenhower?

"He is not!" Wax Johnson yelled from down the bar.

It didn't make sense to Jack either. Dwight D. Eisenhower, Ike, General Eisenhower, was the president of the United States, and before that he had been a five-star general who led America to victory against the Nazis in Europe. It didn't make sense that a five-star general and now the president of the United States would be a Communist, but if Willow said so, then fine.

"Yeah, he is, and I can prove it," Willow said.

Wax dismissed her with a wave and turned back to his conversation with a guy Jack had never seen before. Somebody said he was a new road man for Schlumberger, the big oil field supply outfit out of Houston.

Jack didn't much care if Dwight D. Eisenhower really was a Communist. He had never paid much attention to things like that. He had enough to do with his own life. He left that kind of stuff to Senator, the local drivers' union president, who talked and talked about politics, about Eisenhower and Adlai Stevenson, Allan Shivers and Price Daniel. The nickname Senator didn't really fit because he looked more like a justice of the peace than a senator and talked with the bad grammar and bad words of a deputy sheriff. Not that Jack or anybody else around knew or cared much about what senators looked or talked like.

College was the only one who ever talked to Senator about anything other than union business, and College did it that smart-alecky way he talked to most everyone.

But Jack liked to listen to College, and there, like Refugio, he was, sitting down next to Jack at the bar.

"I hate this place," College said to Jack as he sat down.

"Want to go somewhere else?"

"There is no somewhere else."

Progress said College was the only human being he had ever known who never smiled. Jack said he had seen him do it once when he won a flip for beers at the Tarpon Inn. But Progress didn't believe him. Progress came up with the "College" nickname, and it was not for friendly reasons. He was certain College, whose real name was Anthony Richard Mullett, had never attended one college class, not even in junior college. Progress gave him the name because he acted like he was smarter than everybody, not because he really was.

"Why don't you ever smile?" Jack asked College suddenly, with no thought or warning.

College was a dark-skinned, black-haired man who seemed to Jack to be in his forties, maybe five or so years older than he was himself. But he had been with Great Western for less than ten years.

College did not answer Jack. He spoke to Willow. "A Lone Star and a glass."

"Coming up," she replied.

Jack was also drinking a Lone Star but right out of the bottle, the way most people did at the Tarpon Inn. He had less than half of his left.

"I smile when I'm happy," College said softly to Jack, but still not looking at him. Clearly, he was seldom happy, including right now talking to Jack.

Jack wondered why he liked College at all and why College seemed to take to him in return. Jack knew no more about Anthony Richard Mullett than anyone else did. There had been rumors around that he was the heir to a large dairy company in Kansas City but had been cheated out of his inheritance by somebody connected to the gangsters of the Pendergast machine, who had always been behind the success of Harry Truman. Another story had him being a disrobed Catholic priest who now hated God, Jesus and everyone else. The one that most of the drivers believed was that Anthony Richard Mullett was a rich man's son who couldn't make it in the big world and decided to hide forever behind the steering wheel of a bus. Jack didn't know what to think.

"What did you do before you started driving a bus?" Jack asked. Why not just be direct?

"Nothing."

Jack said, "Everybody did something before they started driving a bus. Everybody did."

"Not me."

"Paul Madison thinks you hate being a bus driver," Jack said to College. "I told him there was no way a man could do a job that he hated."

College took a long sip from his Lone Star but said nothing.

"You didn't come here to talk today, I see," Jack said.

"Not about me or bus driving, that is certainly correct."

Jack had never paid that much attention to the way College actually spoke. Now he did. Now he understood why "College" stuck as a nickname. The way he said "certainly correct" was the way people with smarts and style said it. The *l* and *t* sounds were more distinct than most other people's.

"Did you really go to college for four years?" Jack asked.

"Maybe."

"Thanks for answering me, finally."

"You're welcome."

"What did you study?"

"Anthropology."

"What's that?"

"It's all about where we came from."

"We?"

"You, me, all people everywhere."

"No wonder you took up bus driving."

College looked around and right at Jack and smiled a good one. Jack could hardly wait to tell Progress that he had finally seen a real smile on College's face.

Jack got another Lone Star and a small sack of Tom's Salted Peanuts from Willow.

"Are you hiding from something?" Jack asked College.

"Probably."

Jack decided to move on to the things they usually talked about, which was mostly comparing the steering and other mechanical characteristics of the various buses they drove. College also drove Houston–Corpus overnights, so they both knew the same buses. College shared Jack's amazement over the fact that two buses could come off the assembly line in Chicago or Philadelphia or Muskegon or some place in Ohio but sound and shake and drive as different as if they had come from two different worlds. It was also amazing to both of them that the same bus could drive and react differently to different drivers. For one it acted up and was slow to start, say, but for another it clicked right off.

And after a while Jack told College and Willow and the others that it was time for him to get on a Nueces Transportation bus for home.

—

"How about a movie tonight then?" Loretta had said when he called and said no to lunch.

"Sure," he said.

"Any choice?"

"You say."

She was home by four-thirty and they were at the theater by five. Loretta had picked *Show Boat* to see. She said it was a big musical in Technicolor with lots of good songs and things like that. It had already been out for a couple of years and had come back for a second replay at the Bayside Theater.

Jack was inside the theater, sitting with a sack of popcorn in his lap and watching the opening credits of the movie, before he realized what had happened. Ava was in this movie. Not his Ava but the other one, the movie one, the real one. Ava Gardner.

She was not the main girl star. That was Kathryn Grayson. Ava played a half-Blue singer with a drinking problem who was down on her luck. Jack went furnace-hot inside when she sang a song called "Bill."

He almost cried when, near the end, with black bags under her eyes, she sang "Can't Help Lovin' Dat Man of Mine."

> *Fish gotta swim, birds gotta fly,*
> *I gotta love one man till I die,*
> *Can't help lovin' dat man of mine.*

Loretta did not suggest or even hint about making love when they got home. It was Wednesday. That was what they did on Friday.

Jack had never been happier about that particular habit than he was right then. He had the strange feeling, a really strange feeling, that it would have been disloyal to Ava, his Ava, to make love to Loretta this particular night.

Most of the feelings he was having about everything were strange.

——

Then, going to Houston the next day, he had another animal problem. A woman passenger tried to take a black cocker spaniel on the bus with her at Woodsboro. She said the dog would stay right in her lap all of the way to Ganado, where she was going.

"It's against our rules," he told her.

"He is better behaved than most humans," said the lady, who was a Dollar in her forties.

"I don't make the rules, ma'am."

"He doesn't bite."

"I'm sorry."

"He's completely trained. He will not mess up your bus."

"I'm really sorry."

The woman burst into tears. "I have to go to Ganado!" she screamed. "My mother is dying!"

"I don't make the rules," he said again, wondering this time if she was a checker. Now wouldn't that be something? A checker trying to see if he would give in and let this woman take a dog on a Great Western Trailways bus.

The woman, checker or not and still crying, ran away with her dog under her arm.

"I hate you!" she screamed at him.

And Jack got back up in his bus and drove off toward Houston. He decided there was no way that woman was a checker and he felt bad about her, her cocker spaniel and her mother.

The final episode in his six days and fourteen and a half hours of misery came the next day when he went to the Houston garage to pick up the bus he would drive south to Victoria and Corpus, to Ava, his Ava.

He got in to start it and the engine would not turn over. There was not even a whirl. A mechanic fooled with it for fifteen minutes and pronounced it fixed. But the delay caused him to hurry through all of his prerun preparations at the depot.

The one thing he did not want to be was late into Victoria. He wanted every moment he could possibly have with her.

It was between El Campo and Wharton, with still about ninety minutes to go before Victoria, that he was overcome with panic at the possibility of her not being there.

It was something he had not even considered until then. What if two trips on the 3:15 was it? What if she was not going to be there this Friday?

What if he would never see her again?

Thinking about it caused him to forget to throw off the bundles of the *Houston Press* that were delivered every afternoon by bus to El Campo and Edna.

He also forgot about a passenger who wanted to get off just the other side of Hungerford, a no-depot flag stop. The passenger, a middle-aged woman in a red dress, had to run up the bus aisle and yell at him to stop.

He was embarrassed and apologetic and it started him worrying about himself, but after a while he was back worrying only about whether he would ever see his White Widow again.

—

There, again like Refugio, she was again.

She was the fourth in line and there were another five or six passengers behind her, so there was no way Jack could say anything to her other than "Good to see you again."

"Thank you," she replied.

Good to see you again.

Thank you.

She wore a short-sleeved pink dress. So he felt the bare skin of her elbow for the second time. The touch triggered little shots of something through his fingers up into his arms and down and around and throughout his body. Or maybe he imagined it.

But what did it matter if they were imagined if he really did feel them? And he really did feel something.

It was at Sinton that he knew he had to do something. He could not bear to watch her like this—she was in the sixth-row aisle seat on the left—and think of her slipping away into the Corpus Christi evening before he had asked her a few questions.

Where do you go when you leave the bus depot?

Why do you ride this schedule every Friday?

Will you be back next Friday?

What is your name?

Who are you?

What do you think of me?

Could you love a bus driver?

What about a bus driver who was a Master Operator?

Would you sit in my Angel Seat?

—

The bus depot at Sinton was on the right side of the highway at a Gulf station. Two passengers got off and three got on. He also put off a box of heavy oil-field equipment that had been shipped package express from Haliburton in Houston, and he thumped all four of the rear tires. Company rules required thumping them every two hours or so to see if they were flat. Because they were dual—two on each side of the axle—it was impossible to tell just by looking if one was flat. So the driver thumped them with something heavy and listened to the sound. If the sound was dead, that meant the tire was dead. Jack used his ticket punch for thumping.

He had thumped them in Victoria and did not need to thump them now at Sinton, but he wanted some time to think. Some more time to think.

Ten minutes farther down Highway 77 toward Odem and the intersection with Highway 9 that would take him and his bus and her on into Corpus he made a decision.

He knew that stretch of Highway 9 like the back of his

hand. Like the back of his hand. An uncle, his mother's brother Leroy, who lived up in Floresville near San Antonio, used that expression all the time. After spending a weekend or a summer around that uncle, Jack would come back to Beeville saying it himself. Without thinking about it he saw most things and knew most things and felt most things as clear as if they were the back of his hand.

Just beyond Calallen there was a roadhouse called Smitty's that, like the Tarpon Inn, was popular with some of the bus crowd. Smitty's Seafood Heaven and Earth, it was called officially. One of the Corpus–Laredo drivers met his second wife there, and it was where a Corpus–Brownsville Missouri Pacific driver had been punched out by a drunk sailor who thought the driver had said something about swabbies he did not like. The place had been gutted by a terrible fire several months ago and it was now closed down. Some of the drivers thought the owner, Smitty Mathews, a retired rodeo rider, set the fire for the insurance.

Jack remembered, because he had passed it at least three times a week for the last ten years, that there was an outside telephone booth in the parking lot in front of the now deserted, blackened, forlorn place.

It was a perfect place to have a mechanical breakdown.

One and a half miles before Smitty's he reached down to the dashboard and turned off the ignition. After a beat, he switched it back on. There was a silence and then a pop and then more silence. He kept his foot off the brake, moved the gearshift lever into neutral and let the bus coast.

He pressed the starter. It caught. He gunned it and then switched off the ignition again.

The charred remains of Smitty's Seafood Heaven and Earth was now just ahead. He could see it. He had another hundred yards or so to go. The bus was now moving at about thirty miles an hour. Jack could see a line of four or five cars and trucks stacked up behind him. There was too much oncoming traffic for them to pass him.

He swung the bus into the driveway in front of Smitty's. And he braked her to a full stop.

"Sorry, folks," he said to Ava and the other passengers, "but we have developed some kind of mechanical problem. I am sure we will not be delayed long. Please, everyone, remain onboard the bus. Thank you."

He opened the door and stepped off.

The motor hatch on an ACF-Brill was on the right side of the bus about halfway back. He opened it and reached inside to a piece of wire. He pulled it loose and twisted it.

Then he went back inside the bus, slipped back behind the wheel, turned on the ignition switch, pushed the starter button. He did not have to look into the rearview mirror to know that the ears of every passenger were listening for the sound of the starter and the motor and that the eyes of every passenger were on him.

There was no sound. The starter was not turning over.

He addressed her and the others.

"I see a telephone over there," he said. "We are less than twenty minutes from Corpus. It shouldn't be long before a mechanic or another bus comes to our rescue. Those of you going on to Brownsville or McAllen or Laredo or elsewhere in the Valley have nothing to worry about. All of those connections and things will wait. Please remain on the bus while I go and call. Thank you."

Jennings answered the phone and accepted his collect charges. Jennings was the main daytime dispatcher. Jack told him exactly where he had broken down and described the problem as probably having something to do with the ignition system. Jennings said a bus and a mechanic would be on their way in a few minutes.

"What have you got going on through?" Jennings asked.

"Nine to Raymondville or below, three for Laredo, one of them for Alice," Jack replied.

"We'll hold everything," Jennings said. "Fridays aren't your day, are they, On Time Jack?"

Jack ignored that and said, "There was a problem at the garage in Houston. She wouldn't turn over. A mechanic said he fixed it but you know what that means."

———

There she was inside his bus. He had twenty minutes, maybe twenty-five, to do something, to make a move. But he couldn't just go in and sit down beside her.

Hello, Ava, would you mind if I sit with you while we wait?

I would be delighted, Jack.

You remembered my name!

How could I ever forget?

I love you with all my heart.

I know.

He stepped back into the bus.

"Help is on its way," he announced to her and the other passengers. She was looking right at him. "Please make your-selves comfortable. If you want to get off the bus, that's okay if you'll stay real close—and out of the traffic on the high-way. I want to make sure I deliver all of you in one piece."

Jack heard some laughter. Ava smiled. She obviously thought he, this bus driver, was one clever, funny, witty man.

Yes, but could she love him?

Several of the passengers stood up and started up the aisle toward Jack and the door. That meant he would have to move out of their way so they could get off.

That meant he might as well get off too.

But what if she didn't? What if she stayed right there in her seat?

What if he had done something so irresponsible, stupid and insane as sabotaging his own bus for nothing? What if he had risked his gold badge, his job, his future, his life, for nothing?

Outside now, he lit a Camel.

Jack T. Oliver, you are a fool. You are a lovesick boy. You are not a Master Operator. You are not fit to wear the uniform and carry the ticket punch of a Great Western Trailways bus driver, much less wear the gold badge of a Master Operator.

There she was.

From a spot in the parking lot ten feet away he watched her put her left foot on the scarred concrete and then the other.

He was there by her in two quick steps, two quick seconds. He held out his pack of Camels.

"Would you like a cigarette?" he asked.

"No, thank you," she replied.

"You don't smoke?"

"Not really, no."

A conversation. We are having a conversation!

"This is your third straight Friday with me," he said.

"That's right." She was looking past him. "I assume that phone over there is operational?"

"Yes, ma'am."

Operational. What a terrific word to use. He decided he would use one himself.

"Do you have adequate change?" He loved the word *adequate.*

"Yes, thank you," she replied.

She lowered her incredibly marvelous head, stepped to one side and moved toward the phone booth.

He watched her every step, her every movement. He

watched her put a coin into the slot. He watched her wait while the phone rang at the other end and he watched her talk to someone.

Who was she talking to? A husband, a boyfriend? A mother, a sister? A preacher, a lawyer, a cop?

She hung up. She opened the glass door of the booth and walked toward him and the bus.

"I hope everything is all right," Jack said when she arrived back in his presence.

"Thank you," she said and she kept walking to the bus.

He helped her up.

He saw that the bump was gone from her leg. In the words of Paul Madison, That's progress, you see.

—

At Corpus she disembarked and left him, his bus and the depot the same as before. He tried his best to delay her, but once again, with people lined up behind to get out, it was simply impossible.

"Thanks again" was all he said.

She only smiled.

It was almost twenty minutes later, when he was out of the N.T.C. bus and walking the last two blocks to his house, that he remembered something truly horrible. He had not told her he would not be there next Friday because of the Master Operators dinner in Houston!

He should have stopped her to say: Ava dear, please do not be alarmed when you do not see me next week. I will be getting a gold badge. But I will return the following Friday.

Or something like that.

—

He opened the front door of his house. Loretta was standing just inside.

"What happened?" she asked.

"I had a breakdown on Nine at Calallen."

She was not dressed as she always was. She did not have on a dress or a skirt and blouse or even a pair of slacks. She had on her nightgown. Only her nightgown.

"I put the meat loaf on a very low heat," she said. "But something else is on high boil."

Jack reached out for her. He grabbed her shoulders and kissed her on the lips quickly and without passion.

"Being late like that has really upset me," he said. "I think I'm going to have to take a pass on it—on us, you know what I mean."

"I hear you." But it was obvious from the look on her face that she did not know what he meant.

He did not know either. Not for sure. Not everything. Not even very much.

CHAPTER 7

*T*here had been a lot of stories in the Houston newspapers about the Ben Milam Hotel and its history as the center of Houston's early gambling and whoring industries. Jack had never paid much attention to any of it because by the time it became a part of his own history, as the place he spent his resting layover time, it was just a hotel.

Now, tonight, it was also going to be the place in history where he was presented with his gold Master Operator badge.

It was in one of the big banquet rooms, one named for Stephen F. Austin, who, like Jack's hero, Sam Houston, as well as Ben Milam, Davey Crockett and Mirabeau Lamar (as in the bar down the street), was a big deal in Texas's fight for independence from Mexico. There was a portrait of Austin about the size of a large Great Western bus depot sign on the main wall, behind the head table.

Jack was at that table, along with six other drivers who were getting gold badges and four company executives, including two from the general offices in Dallas.

"I have asked Preacher Williams to say grace over our dinner," said one of the executives into the microphone to get things started. He was Hubert Glisan, the division superintendent in Houston, who always acted as master of ceremonies at these dinners.

Preacher Williams wasn't a preacher, he was a Houston–San Antonio driver who only acted like he was a preacher. College said the closest Preacher, whose real name was Bryan, ever came to Jesus was when he used his name in vain.

"Jesus in heaven, here we are," he prayed. "Here we are, your humble flawed servants, earning our chili and our popcorn of life behind the wheels of our beautiful motorized chariots called buses. Protect us, dear Father, from the sins of the flesh, the hazards of the road, the calamities from your heavens, the temptations of speeding, stealing and loving and of passing on bad rumors about the executives in Dallas. Give us first and last calls to a heavenly home where every run is always on time, help us punch the right tickets, put off the right baggage at the right towns, apply the brakes when we should, stay off the air horn except in emergencies, gear down our engines when we should and swerve to avoid head-ons when we should. In your name and that of Great Western Trailways, the route of the Silversides Thruliners, the Always Going Your Way company which is the Easiest Travel on Earth to the Next Town or Across America, we pray. Amen."

Jack figured it was good Preacher Williams decided on being a bus driver because he would never have made it as a real preacher. Although College said in his tight way that Preacher was actually more interesting than any real one he had ever heard. Jack agreed with that. At one dinner Jack went to, Preacher Williams handed out mimeographed copies of what he said was "The Operator's Creed," which he had everyone read out loud together. It had things in it about "Transporting People Is My Business," "The Safety of My Passengers Is My First Concern," and "Courtesy to Passengers Is My Practice. The people who ride with me provide my livelihood. I will treat them with great respect."

Mr. Glisan told everyone to go ahead and eat.

Jack put some butter on a warm dinner roll, took a sip of iced tea and cut into the veal cutlet on the plate before him. It was the first Friday night in a while that he had not eaten Loretta's meat loaf. It was the second Friday night in a row that he had not made love to Loretta.

"I never thought I'd ever be up here," said Sunshine Ashley, sitting on Jack's right. Sunshine, the man so called because he was just the opposite of sunshine. "I figured I'd fry in a head-on, get blown away by an Indianola or get caught by a checker before this would happen."

"I always knew I'd get the gold badge someday," Jack said.

"Me, too," said the guy on the other side of Jack. He was Dippy Doolittle, a Houston–Dallas driver who got the name Dippy because he was. Jack had been told a hundred times about the Saturday night Dippy was driving down U.S. 75 south from Corsicana in a rainstorm when he mistakenly turned right off on State Highway 14 and was in Mexia, which was twenty-two miles west of his route, before he realized what he had done. Sunshine, on the other hand, had a spotless driving record. But here they were, one thinking he would make it to Master Operator, the other not. Jack decided it was just another sign of how different people were, and putting a Great Western Trailways uniform on them did not change the differences all that much.

What it took to qualify was twelve years without a chargeable accident, plus what was called "an exemplary record of attention to duty," which meant whatever the company decided it meant. Guys who showed up too much in dirty or unpressed uniforms, who were caught smoking a lot while driving or not wearing their caps while loading or unloading passengers, or who habitually ran late did not make it. There were several drivers in the system, five or six Jack knew personally, who had more than twenty years of driving time but were still wearing silver badges and probably always would. They had never done anything bad enough to get fired but they would never be good enough to be Master Operators.

There were a hundred and fifty or so people eating in groups of eight or ten at round tables out in the room. Most were drivers, dispatchers and people like that. Some were in civilian clothes, coats and ties, but most, like Jack and the other honorees, were in uniform.

"Have you heard about the checkers?" Sunshine said to Jack.

"I've always heard about the checkers," Jack said.

"They're sending hundreds this time," Sunshine said. "Hundreds. I told you they're out to get us all. Well, they are. All of us. Every damned one of us."

"Think about that, Sunshine. Why would the company want to get all of its drivers. Who in the hell would drive their buses?"

"That's exactly what I'm asking."

"Well, the answer is nobody. They would have nobody to drive their buses if they got all of us."

"That's what I say, and it makes me sick and afraid to think about it."

"Don't think about it."

"I can't help it."

"You never do anything wrong anyhow, so no checker could catch you doing anything anyhow."

"It'll make 'em work twice as hard and as long until they do catch me."

"You're a crazy man, Sunshine."

"They might even plant something on me. You still doing that Christmas thing?"

"Yep."

"There's a big wooden Santa Claus out in a field this side of Bloomington," Sunshine said. "You interested?"

"How big?"

"As you and me."

"Is it for sale?"

"I don't know. You want me to check it out?"

"Yep."

"I hate even putting up a tree in my living room. They cause fires, you know. You ever had a fire with all of that stuff you have?"

"Never."

"Be careful."

"I am."

Mr. Glisan called for everybody's attention, saying it was all right to go ahead and finish the chocolate cake and have some coffee while they went on with the program.

He then started the speaking off with some words of encouragement about the future.

He said: "I don't think I have to tell you-all that the people aren't riding our buses like they used to. They're not riding Greyhound and our other competitors' buses like they used to either. I also don't have to tell you why. It's all those cars out there. You operators see them on the roads and highways and streets. They are our real competition. They are the enemy. We are meeting that enemy with advertising and publicity that stresses the safety of bus transportation, the avoidance of prohibitive parking charges in larger cities and the absence of driver-tension characteristics for bus passengers. It is not working that well so far. The people are still buying and driving and riding in cars. However, when the saturation point of private vehicular traffic on our highways and streets is reached, it will begin to bear fruit.

"As times goes by I believe more and more people will use public transportation when they realize the menace that is abroad on our highways today in the form of overpowered autos driven by people who drive and act as though safety is the responsibility of the other fellow. I hope the waiting period will not be too long. But I assure you we of Great Western Trailways will still be here, providing the best transportation on our particular part of God's green earth, when the people get out of their cars and come back to the buses, where they belong."

Everybody gave Mr. Glisan a round of hoots and applause.

Then he said that the bad part of the waiting was that there would be no money to buy new buses for a while. "I know our ACFs are growing old and cranky but we're all going to have to get used to having them around as the mainstay of our mainline runs for a while longer," he said. Some of the drivers let out some groans. Not Jack. As far as he was concerned, it would not matter if they never replaced the ACF-Brills. That bus was, in his opinion, the best there was or would ever be.

"I also know that some of you will miss the great life of going after new equipment, but we all have to adjust to life as it is," said Mr. Glisan. One of the privileges of being a Master Operator was going to big cities like Chicago and Philadelphia at company expense, taking delivery on a new bus at the factory and then driving back to Texas. Jack had heard the stories about thick steaks and french fries and apple cobbler and nice hotels at company expense.

Mr. Glisan turned the microphone over to Rex Al Barney, Great Western's chief operator and director of operator training. Pharmacy, as he was called because Rex and Al went together to form Rexall, was the most feared and most loved man in the system. Like Paul Madison, he had started at the beginning with the bus business. He was a driver for the old Wichita Falls–Fort Worth Coaches, a company that was known mostly for painting the fronts of its buses like they were jackrabbit faces with the headlights as the eyes, the front bumpers as mouths, the running lights as ears and so on.

Pharmacy, who had the power to fire any driver for just about anything, resembled an old football player and was the best public speaker in the Great Western Trailways system. Jack had heard him talk at safety meetings and dinners several times.

Jack, along with everyone else in the room, was grinning before Pharmacy even opened his mouth.

Pharmacy thanked Mr. Glisan and assured him that the Great Western operators stood ready to do their part to help the company get over what he called "this stupid craziness about the car that has bit the minds and other parts of so many of our customers."

Then to the audience he said: "It's always a pleasure to be in the company of so many of my fellow bus drivers. That's what we all are, even if in the fancy language of the company now we are called operators. I thought an operator was some pretty little lady who gave you the phone number you were looking for. Or somebody in a white coat and a mustache who stuck a knife in my stomach and pulled out an appendix."

Jack and everybody laughed.

"I am always asked what it takes to be a bus operator, a

bus driver. You know, the qualifications for employment. Not the ones about being so tall and so smart and so unfat and so able to get a driver's license and so physically fit and so able to see the road ahead. I mean the real qualifications. The personal qualifications. Well, I finally after all these years found them written down. They were in a magazine put out for the employees of Tri-State Trailways over in Louisiana and Mississippi. All it says is that a guy named Smokey wrote it. I don't know who Smokey is.

"But here's what he said about the kind of man a bus driver must be.

"He must be a man of vision and ambition, an after-dinner speaker, a before- and after-dinner entertainer, a night owl—work all day, drive all night and appear fresh the next day. He must be a man who can learn to sleep on the floor and eat two meals a day to economize on traveling expenses so he can entertain his friends in the next town.

"He must be able to entertain passengers, wives, sweeties and pet waitresses without becoming too amorous. He must inhale dust, drive through snow twelve feet deep at ten below and work all summer without perspiring or acquiring B.O.

"He must be a man's man, a ladies' man, a model husband, a fatherly father, a devoted son-in-law, a good provider, a plutocrat, Democrat, Republican, a New Dealer and fast dealer—a technician, electrician, politician, polytechnician, mechanist, mechanic, polygamist and ambidextrous.

"He must attend labor union meetings, tournaments, funerals and births and visit all passengers in hospitals and jails once a month.

"He must have a wide range of telephone numbers of all principal cities and villages when entertaining the traffic department.

"He must be an expert driver, talker, liar, dancer, traveler, bridge player, poker hound, toreador, golf player, diplomat, financier, capitalist and philanthropist—and an authority on palmistry, chemistry, archaeology, psychology, physiology, meteorology, redheads and lingerie.

"That's what this guy Smokey had to say, and from my driver's seat it seems to me he's got it about right. What do you-all think?"

Jack was laughing so hard he was crying. So was everyone else.

"Now you know what we're looking for when we interview prospects. And now you know what these seven hotshots up here at the head table did to get all of this special attention here tonight."

Pharmacy moved toward getting serious. He talked about how the operator, the driver, was the backbone as well as the tailbone of Great Western Trailways. He said it was the experience the passenger has with the operator that will ultimately decide whether that passenger gets off a Great Western bus a happy or an unhappy customer.

"The Great Western name and future are in our hands now more than ever, along with the steering wheel of an ACF-Brill, Beck, Aerocoach or Flxible Clipper."

Jack and the others applauded. Jack knew everything Pharmacy was saying was absolutely true, but it was good to hear it from somebody like Pharmacy. Of course, he was one of them himself, even if he was a big executive now. Once a bus driver, always a bus driver, in the mind if nowhere else.

He wondered if Ava would be more pleased with him if he became an executive, like Pharmacy.

I would hate it, dearest Ava.

Why, dear Jack?

I love being a bus driver, I love being a backbone as well as a tailbone of Great Western. I don't think I could give up the open road.

Not even for me, dear Jack?

Let me think about it, dearest Ava.

"Now we come to the real reason we are all here tonight," Pharmacy said. "There are seven reasons. I will call them to come forward here one at a time to receive their gold badges, signifying that they have met the highest standards we have, to achieve the highest rank we have here at Great Western Trailways—that of Master Operator."

It was done alphabetically. That put Jack next to last.

"Jack T. Oliver of Corpus Christi!" said Pharmacy when the time came. "The man we all know and love as On Time."

For a split second he felt like a movie star getting an Academy Award. The closest thing to it in his life before was receiving his first letter in football for the Beeville High Trojans. He never started, but he got into every game as a guard from his junior year on. He still had the blue letter jackets with the big white *B*s on them, and when he thought about those days he was able to see himself playing quarterback and throwing winning touchdowns in bi-district championship games.

The badge-changing ceremony was simple. Jack and the other six had already removed their regular silver-and-red badges from their caps.

"Here is your badge, Jack," Pharmacy said at the microphone. "Congratulations."

Jack shook Pharmacy's hand and then took the badge. There, as five of the others had already done, he undid the little screws on the back of the gold badge and then stuck it onto the front of his cap where it belonged.

He looked hard at the badge as he did it. It was a beautiful thing, with the words "Great Western Trailways" encircling a map of the United States at the top of the shield, and the words "Master Operator" right below. He had seen it on Progress Paul and a few others for years. Now it would be on him. Where it belonged.

He put on his cap. There was much applause.

He would have given anything for Ava to be there to see him, to see this. It would have made her see what a substantial and important and meaningful thing driving a bus really was.

Look at this badge, Ava. I am no longer just an ordinary bus driver, an ordinary man. I am a Master Operator. I am now worth loving.

——

As the dinner was breaking up a few minutes later, Pharmacy came over to say a final good-bye and good night to each of the new Master Operators.

"And how's it going for you, Jack?" he asked when he got to Jack.

"Just great, Pharmacy, just great."

"I see the weight's still off."

That made Jack mad. It was a completely unnecessary thing to say. He hadn't had a weight problem in more than seven or eight years. All he said was "My looks speak for themselves, Pharmacy."

"That's right. What's happening to you on Fridays, Jack?"

Jack felt his body quiver. "Fridays?"

"I was looking at some log reports this afternoon with Hubert. You were out of Victoria on time but late into Corpus three Fridays in a row. That is something for our man On Time Jack."

"Last Friday I had a breakdown."

"Right. Something happened to the ignition wire."

"Yeah. I think it was bad when I left Houston. I had trouble getting it out of the garage."

"I read that. You missed throwing off some papers one Friday."

"Now I do not know what happened on that. I really do not . . ."

"And an agent said you forgot a passenger?"

Forgot a passenger? "I don't know about that."

"She was going to Hungerford, if my memory serves."

"Oh, right. Her."

"Well, again, good luck and congratulations. You are one of our best."

Jack thanked him and Pharmacy moved on to talk to someone else.

———

Jack ran into Horns Livingston in the hotel lobby. He was looking for somebody to go to the movies with him.

"I guess you're not interested in my kind of movie, are you Master Operator Oliver? Congratulations, by the way."

"Thanks and thanks," Jack said. "I *am* interested." And he smiled and nodded and walked out the front door of the Milam with Horns Livingston in the direction of the Lone Star Majestic Theater.

———

The movie, *Lovesick Spies Blues,* was not even in color. It opened with a shot of a guy in a light-colored raincoat waiting under a lamppost on a brick-paved street. "Lisbon, 1944," it said underneath. He smoked a cigarette and looked around and smoked another cigarette and looked around again. Somebody was supposed to meet him, obviously. They were late. He was worried.

Then there was the sound of high heels hitting the bricks. He turned in the direction from whence it came. And there she was. A blond woman in a dark cloth coat. She looked scared and sad. They extended their arms to each other and embraced. They spoke, but Jack could not understand what they were saying. It was in French.

"Dearest," the subtitle said at the bottom of the screen.

"My darling," it said right afterward.

Both gave startled looks. There was the sound of boot heels on the bricks.

"Someone's coming!" said the subtitle.

The man and the woman put up the collars on their coats and walked away together. After a few seconds they started running. The sound of the boot heels on the bricks remained, getting louder and then fainter. Finally the sound stopped as the pair stopped running at the entrance to a large park. They hugged and went into the park. In a few seconds they were surrounded by bushes.

He removed his coat and placed it on the ground. He assisted her to the ground with a touch to the elbow not unlike the one Jack used to help Ava and other passengers on and off his bus.

He joined her on his coat.

"This must be the last time," she said in the subtitle.

"I know," he said. "But I would rather die."

"We will both die if we continue."

"It is then only a matter of how and when I die, my dearest."

"For me as well."

They kissed. He removed her dark cloth coat. He ran his right hand through her hair and over her shoulders. He put his head down on her chest.

"Why must our nations be at war, Jacques?" she said.

"It is a matter for history, not for people who love one another, Maria."

"We Italians should not have done what we did."

"We French had no choice but to do what we did."

"I know, my dear Jacques, I know. But I am first and always an Italian. I must serve my country."

"But it is Fascist."

"I know, but it is my country."

"But you are stealing secrets. You are a spy."

"So are you."

"But for a just cause, to defeat fascism."

He unbuttoned her blouse.

"I must," he said.

"I know," she said.

Her breasts were exposed. He kissed each one fervently.

"Oh, why must we be enemies?" she asked.

"It is in our blood," he said after coming up for air.

"So is our love."

"It is our blood that will be spilled."

He removed his suit coat, tie and shirt.

And so it went for over an hour. Full intercourse was never quite shown but most everything else was. Jack had heard of movies like this but this was the first time he had ever seen one.

He had felt dirty and stupid when he first came into the lobby. He did not look at either the woman who sold the tickets or the young man who took them at the door. It was pitch-black inside the theater itself and that was just fine with Jack. It took a few seconds to get used to the dark in order to find a seat but he didn't mind.

"I like to sit right down front," Horns said.

"Not me," said Jack. "I'm a back-of-the-theater man."

"All right," said Horns. "I'll see you when it's over."

And when it was over he went out into the lobby and waited for Horns.

Both of the spies, Maria as well as Jacques, did not survive. She was arrested and then tortured in a hotel room by a

Gestapo officer in plainclothes. He wanted to know every-thing she had told her French lover. She repeatedly claimed she told him nothing, but the Nazi did not believe her. He had two hoods take her to a cliff overlooking an ocean and throw her several hundred feet to her death.

Jacques died in a gun battle with the Gestapo hoods after he arrived at the cliff seconds too late to save the woman he loved.

"Our love was not to be," he said as he lay bleeding to death.

Jack left the theater wondering if, and hoping that, the turn-on he had received from watching Jacques and Maria would last until he came home to Loretta the next day.

But it was gone by the time he got back to the hotel and into his room.

He went to sleep thinking about Ava and vowing to try again in the morning on the way back to Corpus to see if he could bring back Maria and Jacques.

CHAPTER 8

The custom and practice among Great Western Trailways drivers was to flash their bus headlights at each other when approaching from opposite directions. One flick meant simply Hi and all is well. Two flicks meant Hi and look out for a speed trap, an accident or some other hazard up ahead. Three flicks meant Stop, I need to talk to you.

The next morning between Ganado and Edna, Jack flicked three times at the oncoming bus from Victoria, Corpus and the Valley. College was driving it. There had been a lot of swapping of runs and bringing in of extra-board people to accommodate the needs of drivers like Jack to be at the Master Operator dinner in Houston. College was the guy who had ended up driving Jack's run south the previous day.

"I need a couple of cash fare receipts," Jack said to College. Jack had stopped his bus on the westbound shoulder of the highway and dashed across to College, whose bus was on the other shoulder.

"I cannot believe the new Master Operator went off without something like that," said College. He stepped up into his bus and returned in a minute with a whole book of cash fare receipts.

"Congratulations, by the way, Jack," he said. "Let me look at it."

College was an inch or so taller than Jack. He stepped up to look right at the gold badge on Jack's hat. "A thing of beauty," he said. "If things don't work out you can melt it down and sell it for gold. Well, got to be on our way."

Jack had the sad thought—the sad *certain* thought—that College Tony Mullett would never get a gold badge. Nobody who never smiled could ever become a Master Operator.

"How did it go on my run yesterday?" Jack asked quickly, trying his best to appear casual, normal, nonchalant.

"Same as always."

"Did you happen to pick up a passenger in Victoria who looked sick?"

"Sick? No, not that I remember. There were only five or six. A couple of Mexicans and a few others. Everybody looked well. Look, we both need to get a move on."

"Nobody asked about me there in Victoria?"

"Progress Paul. He talked about how wonderful it was that you got your gold badge and all. Said it was progress, you see."

"I mean the passengers."

"Jack, come on. Like I said, there were two Mexicans. The only other passenger I remember was some looker of a woman, a White Widow type. She sure as hell didn't ask about you. I kept wishing she would ask about me. I couldn't keep my eyes off of her. But that was it. Did you hear about Texas Red Rocket?"

"What about it?"

"One of the dispatchers found their section torn out of

Mr. Glisan's copy of the Red Guide." The Red Guide was the two-inch-thick book with a red cover that contained all the schedules of all the intercity bus companies in the United States and Canada. Its real name was *Russell's Official National Motor Coach Guide.*

"So what?"

"Well, they're saying it may mean we're buying 'em out. I heard at the Tarpon yesterday that now they think Truman was a Commie, too. Nixon said it to somebody."

"Why would he say something like that?"

"I was surprised Ike kept him on the ticket. Should have dumped him. Bye for now, Jack."

Dump Nixon? Truman too? "Right. Thanks." Preacher Williams's prayer line about rumors was right on target. They traveled up and down the lines of Great Western Trailways like electricity through the air.

College jumped back into his bus and in a few seconds they were gone.

And a couple of seconds after that Jack and his bus were going the other way.

He could not imagine why Ava had not asked about him. He might have been hurt, sick or even dead. And she did not ask.

It could be that she was simply too shy, too embarrassed to ask.

———

The sex thing was really not working. Horns Livingston's device for maintaining himself sexually ready for his wife back in Shreveport was not having the same effect on Jack. Try as he did to keep the spies Jacques and Maria in his mind, he could not. Not enough, at least. And when he did it was Ava who was Maria, not Loretta.

The new gold badge on his cap got in the way also. All

along the route the agents had nice things to say to him about his being made a Master Operator. Those in Louise, Wharton and El Campo insisted on having somebody take their pictures with Jack in front of his bus.

He had also had to cope with Lem Odum, a retired Rosenberg High School civics and English teacher who traveled regularly from Rosenberg to Victoria to get his back adjusted by the only woman chiropractor in South Texas. "Men don't know how to do it," he had explained to Jack many trips ago. "They're too rough, too impatient, too stupid."

As always, Lem, who was probably seventy-five years old and who always wore white pants and white leather shoes, insisted on sitting in Jack's Angel Seat and talking a mile a minute.

"You know how all these towns got their names, don't you, Mr. Oliver? Yes, I am sure you do. This highway follows the route of the old New York, Texas and Mexico Railways, which was owned by an Italian count named Telfener and his American father-in-law, named Hungerford. They called it the Macaroni Line and it only got built for ninety miles from Rosenberg to Victoria. But it left its mark. They named two towns after themselves, Telfener and Hungerford, plus a couple for Telfener's daughters, Inez and Edna, and two more after a partner, John Mackay, and his daughter, Louise. You already knew all of that, didn't you, Mr. Oliver. Very interesting history along this highway. You should tell the passengers about it as you drive along. They would love knowing where they are going and who went before them . . ."

He was delighted when he finally got to Victoria, where the schedule called for a full twenty-five-minute noon-meal rest stop. He arrived to some real commotion. Progress Paul, Johnny Merriweather and the porter, Willie Church, were standing there in the depot driveway. Each was holding a handmade sign. MASTER OLIVER IS OUR MAN was the message on Paul's.

"Lunch is on me," said Paul to Jack, "if you don't have more than a hamburger."

A hamburger all the way with fries was exactly what Jack ate.

"I hold my glass up in your honor," said Paul, holding up a cup of coffee, which, as far as Jack ever saw, was the only thing Paul Madison ever drank.

Jack clinked his iced-tea glass against Paul's cup and against cups or glasses held by two other drivers at the table. One was an extra-board man waiting to double a schedule back to Houston at three o'clock. The other drove the Austin–Victoria turnaround for Texas Red Rocket Motorcoaches. He, like Paul, was on a layover.

Jack entertained them for a few minutes with a little bit of what he could remember of Pharmacy's spiel about what it took to be a bus driver. And he told them about Sunshine, sitting up there about to get his gold badge but worried that the same company that was giving it to him also was looking for ways to fire him.

"Well, the checkers are out, he is sure right about that," Paul said.

"How do you know that?" Jack asked.

"I hauled one of them this morning."

"Now, come on, Paul, how did you know it was a checker."

"A guy in dirty overalls about thirty flagged me down just down the road from Sample, between Smiley and Westhoff. He said he was going to Cuero and gave me a twenty-dollar bill. He was a checker."

"How do you know that?"

"Because I know everybody by sight and by name who lives anywhere near Sample and he wasn't one of them who does. He was a setup. Nobody in there would have a twenty-dollar bill in their pocket either."

"Well, you don't have anything to worry about."

"Nope."

Neither do I, thought Jack. I am no Sunshine. I know for sure Great Western Trailways needs me and Paul and our kind to stay in business. Like Pharmacy said about the backbone and the tailbone. What good were buses without drivers?

A few minutes later when he loaded up for Corpus he did pay particularly close attention to each and every one of the eleven passengers who got onboard. Maybe, just maybe, one of them was a checker. But then he thought, So what? I have nothing to fear from any checker.

He also could not help but look in the line of passengers for her, for Ava. Of course it was Saturday morning instead of Friday afternoon, and of course she had already gone to Corpus the day before with College. She was clearly "the looker" he was talking about.

But he still could not help but look and hope.

Would he spend the rest of his life looking and hoping for another sight of her?

———

"What's suddenly wrong with me, Jack?"

"Nothing."

"Don't say 'nothing' like that," Loretta said.

"I don't know any other way to say it."

"You said it like it was a secret."

" 'Nothing' is not a secret."

"You're fooling around with somebody," Loretta said.

"That's the secret. It turns out you're just like every other
bus driver in the world, that's the secret. You can't keep your
hands off of women, you can't keep your thing in your pants.
You're nothing but a bus driver after all. Nothing but a
bus driver who thinks promises to your wife don't count,
only hers to you do. Nothing but a little boy bus driver.
That's what you are, Jack. You lose a few pounds, get that
uniform so it fits and you decide you are ready to go out
there and have yourself some women, to hell with me, to hell
with what you swore to do in front of that Methodist
preacher and your mommy and daddy and my mommy and
daddy and before Jesus and God and everyone else in that
church. You no-good rotten bastard. You may have a gold
badge from Great Western Trailways but you do not have a
gold badge from life, I can tell you that. You are a lowlife,
Jack. You are not a Master Operator person. You are not
a gold badge person. You are not. You are not. You think
you are skinny and that makes you a lover. You think you
are skinny and that makes you a ladykiller. You think you are
skinny and that makes you irresistible. You think you are skinny and that makes you something you are not. You are not
any of that, Jack. You are still the same Jack. Nothing has
changed just because you can wear pants with a thirty-four
waist instead of a forty-two. Nothing has changed because
you can wear a shirt with a sixteen collar instead of a seventeen and a half. Nothing has changed, Jack, except the core
of your soul. And that smells. I can smell it. It is rotten. It is
really rotten."

They were sitting at the kitchen table, the only place they
sat and talked about important things. This was the most
important thing they had ever talked about or probably ever
would talk about.

The amazing thing to Jack was that Loretta was not

screaming it out. Her words were screams but her voice was quiet. He waited for her to stop, and when she did, he looked off at the refrigerator for a while.

"Say something, Jack," Loretta said. "Say anything, Jack."

"I'm not fooling around," Jack said. "I am not fooling around."

"Why did you say it twice like that? Mr. Harte at the paper always says if somebody says something twice they are lying. The second time is to convince themselves they aren't. It's like they are quoting themselves and that makes it all true because the quoting is true. I did not kill the butcher. I did not kill the butcher. The first time was a lie. The second time wasn't because it was just repeating, quoting the first time. And it is true I said it once, so that makes quoting it true."

"That doesn't make sense."

"It makes more than you do, coming in here now saying again—again saying—you don't think you are up to making love to your wife, me, the woman you say you love."

"I strained my back throwing some express off the bus at Wharton. I told you I strained my back throwing some express off the bus at . . ."

"There you go, lying again."

Jack really was lying. He was lying in a way that he had never done before to Loretta. His back was fine, of course. The only express he had to put off at Wharton was a small box of auto parts for the Chevrolet dealer.

"Let me tell you about the dinner at the Milam," he said.

"Go ahead, tell me. I really want to hear about how the great Master Operator got his great gold badge. Was she there?"

"Who?"

"Her."

"Her?"

"You know who I mean."

Yes, he knew who she meant, but she didn't know. Nobody knew what was going on in his mind. Nobody knew that. Only he knew that. That was the only private place there was in a person's life. The mind. He knew who she meant and only he knew. Loretta did not know.

He described the Milam Hotel meeting room and what Mr. Glisan and Pharmacy said. Loretta did not crack a smile, even when he repeated a little bit of Preacher Williams's stupid prayer.

"Was she there, Jack, is still my question."

"My question is still Who?"

"Your girlfriend."

"I don't have a girlfriend."

"I don't hear you, Jack."

"Then you're not listening."

"I offer to reward my new Master Operator with anything and as much as he wants and what does he say? He says no thanks, because he strained his back putting off some express at Wharton. He says it twice the first time and then he says it twice again. That to me means only one thing and that one thing is that he has a girlfriend. I hear you. Let's go to the movies, then."

"Great. Let's do."

She stood up. "See what I mean?"

"What are you talking about?"

"You didn't say that twice. You said 'Great' and 'Let's do' only once. That means you were not lying. You really think it's greater to go to a movie with me than to make love with me."

"I'm going to go change clothes."

"You don't want to wear your new gold badge to the movies?"

He did not answer her and walked on out of the kitchen toward their bedroom.

"Does she have a name, Jack? Does this girlfriend of yours have a name? Is she a ticket agent or what? A passenger or what? Have you got her swooning because of that uniform, Jack? Mr. Sexy Thin Jack T. Oliver, Master Operator."

He wasn't sure how much longer he could go on like this.

He vaguely remembered that as a line from the movie about the two spies. They didn't know how much longer they could go on and they didn't go on much longer because they died.

And for the first time since they met at that Nueces Transportation party, he thought about Loretta dying. He wondered what the preacher who married them would say about her before the pallbearers, all Great Western drivers in uniform, carried her out in a coffin to be buried at the Resthaven Cemetery on Highway 9 on the road to Odem.

He saw himself sitting there in the front row, his eyes closed, his head down, while somebody played on an organ "I Walk Through the Valley Alone," Loretta's favorite hymn. He didn't look at Loretta's parents there in the pew to his right. They came over from Ingleside, a small fishing town across the bay to the east from Corpus. That was where Loretta had grown up and where her father, Marsh Lindsey, still ran a small bait-and-tackle store in a marina. Loretta's cousin, Alice Armstrong, the All-American Girl, was in the pew with the Lindseys, along with Mr. Harte and several of the girls from the *Caller*. Jack had asked his own mother and father not to come from Beeville to the funeral and they honored his request. He seldom thought of them as part of his life anymore. The Great Western drivers and dispatchers and ticket agents and porters were his family now. They were the ones who really mattered to him.

He saw himself with his head in Ava's lap. He was in full

uniform and he was crying. She was patting him on the top of his uniform cap.

"Now, now, Jack," Ava said. "It wasn't your fault. You must not punish yourself this way."

"It was my fault," he said between the sobs.

"Now, now, Jack," Ava said, removing his cap and running her fingers through his hair. "How could you have known she didn't know how to run out of a house on fire?"

He hoped and prayed Loretta didn't want to see *Show Boat* again tonight.

—

Jack had done only a few things in his life that made him feel ashamed. Like everybody else in the world, he had told a few lies, particularly to his parents and to teachers when he was growing up, but none that did serious or permanent harm to anyone else. He had stolen a bamboo fishing rod out of the garage of a neighbor in Beeville, but he returned it out of guilt after he had used it only once. He had used a cheat sheet taped to the inside of his wrist to answer four of seventeen questions on a geometry exam when he was a senior in high school. As a grown-up in Corpus, when he was given change from a ten-dollar bill instead of a five by mistake at the post office, he had kept it. He had screamed cuss words at strangers and belched and expended gas in public places a few times. But overall, he had very few reasons to feel deep shame, the kind that lingered in the soul for more than a week or put people to bed or out of their heads. He hadn't even done that much in his imagination to be ashamed of.

Now, suddenly, at the age of thirty-six in the year 1956, after just becoming a Master Operator, he was thinking about the death of Loretta, and thinking about it as a good thing.

The shame of it made him shudder and ache down inside

below his stomach, as happened sometimes when he drove his car over the Highway 281 high bridge that went east from downtown over the ship channel to the Port of Corpus Christi.

And he spoke to himself:

It's an unbelievable situation. I am acting like a high school boy in jeans and boots with a crew cut and a letter jacket. I have to stop this. I cannot continue to moon about this woman, this woman I call Ava. How silly that is. Here I am, talking about this stranger as if she was my girlfriend or mistress or something or other. Mistress. Listen to me use that word. What exactly is a mistress anyhow? I don't even know her name! I call her Ava after a movie star. I remember guys in high school in Beeville did that. They'd come home from a movie with Hedy Lamarr or Lana Turner in it and then on Saturday night, on dates with real girls, they'd imagine they were actually kissing or feeling up Hedy or Lana. Grown-up Master Operators do not act that way. But here I am. I mean, here I am. My wife. What have I done to her? She asks if I am running around on her? No, I say. Which is the truth. The technical truth. But I am running way, way around on her in my head. And then some. But I cannot tell her that. I cannot say, Loretta dear, what I am doing, to tell the truth, is that I have fallen like heavy rain on dry sand for a woman on my Friday bus. We have exchanged maybe twenty words. Forty words, counting both the ones she has said and the ones I have said. Forty words! She looks at me like she does not even really see me. And that is probably because she really doesn't. I am only the bus driver. I am like the seat. Oh my, there is the bus seat. Oh my, there is the bus driver. She didn't even miss me last Friday. Or at least if she did, she didn't say anything to College. "Where is that wonderful man Jack T. Oliver, the regular driver on this run? Is he down with the flu? Did he have to have an operation to remove something? Is he on vacation? Where did he go on vacation? Did he die? Did he get run over by another bus? Has he become president of Great Western Trailways? Has he become a movie star? Is he Ward Bond?" But not a word like any of that. Not one question. This cannot go on. I cannot continue to let this do this to me. Do what to me? Well, look what happened last Friday. I actually sabotaged a bus. I actually destroyed company property so I could simply be with her another twenty-five minutes or so. I sabotaged a bus! It was simply crazy. Am I simply crazy? I am not thinking about murder, heavens no, but I am thinking about Loretta dying. By natural causes, by all means. In a fire, of all things. I cannot believe it! I am thinking that if she died, then Ava would hold my head in her lap and comfort me. Ava would make it all better for me. If Loretta were dead then everything would be all right. Then what I am thinking about Ava would be fine, would be all right, would be honorable, would be clean. You are a terrible, rotten despicable person, Jack T. Oliver. I am ashamed to be you.

Jack said all of this to himself that night as he lay next to Loretta. They had seen *High Noon* with Gary Cooper and Grace Kelly. Now Loretta was asleep. He had faked being asleep, but when he was sure she was, he opened his eyes and went to the kitchen for a glass of water.

He wanted to think. And he wanted to talk. He wanted to say what he had to say to somebody. But there was nobody to talk to. He had almost started with Progress Paul Madison but that was not going to work. What about College? Maybe he really was smart, maybe he really did go through four years of college. Maybe he would listen and understand and help. And help. Help. Help was what he needed, all right, and maybe all that help needed to be was for somebody to listen to him tell his story, recite his awfulness, admit his shame. But there was nobody. There was nobody. There was nobody he could tell about Ava on the bus and what she was doing to him.

Some things are too private. Some thoughts are too shameful to have, much less to talk to someone else about. How can a normal person go around talking about having a fantasy love affair in the head with a woman who didn't even miss him when College drove the schedule? How could a normal person go around talking about wishing his wife was dead in a fire in his own house?

But there are some things that seem too important not to talk out loud about. It's not enough to just think to yourself about them. They have to be spoken.

Jack wished he had a friend he could call.

"Hey, Kenny, this is Jack. I need to talk to you about something important right now, this very minute. I know it's three A.M. and you live in Kingsville, thirty miles away, but I need you. Okay?"

"Okay, Jack. I'll be right there."

But there was no Kenny in Kingsville in Jack's life. Was there a Kenny in Kingsville in everybody else's life? Do other people know people so well that they could call them in the middle of the night and get them to come over to hear about a crazy thing like his love affair with a woman named Ava on his bus? A woman named Ava whose name was really something else? /

Does Loretta have somebody she can talk to? Somebody she can tell about what her husband, Jack, is acting like? Which is like he has a girlfriend. Is there someone she can tell about the fact that her husband has suddenly given up making love to her either before or after the meat loaf?

No, probably not. There are some things that we just

cannot talk to anybody about. It's the same for everybody. Or maybe it isn't. Maybe it's just for men.

Thoughts about wanting your parents to leave you or your Spanish teacher to come over and unzip your fly or being tempted to yell something terrible in the middle of the Sears store or wanting to walk into the grocery store that wouldn't cash your check and blow up the manager with a twelve-gauge shotgun.

Nobody talks about those kinds of things with anybody.

So maybe Ava will have to stay unspoken about to anyone.

So that meant he was on his own, just as he always had been, and as far as he knew, just like everybody else was, too. But knowing that everybody else was did not help one bit. It even made it worse.

CHAPTER 9

*T*he rain began between El Campo and Wharton. At first it was only a few drops on the windshield. But he could tell almost from the start that it was going to be a bad one, much worse than the simple straight-down rain that had come the week before on his day off, even worse than what they said in the forecast.

Jack turned on the ACF-Brill's huge wipers and a few minutes later he turned on the headlights and the running lights. Some wind came up east of Ganado and it was blowing the rain sideways across the highway by the time he got to Edna. He put on a yellow slicker and used a large black umbrella to help passengers keep dry as they dashed off or onto the bus. The slicker and the umbrella were part of the equipment supplied by the company.

All of that took valuable time. Traffic was also slower than usual. It always was when it rained heavily. The dispatcher in

Houston had told him to expect heavy rain and maybe even a thunderstorm or two. He said the forecast said it was part of a whipping tail of a tropical storm, a real Indianola, that had stalled somewhere out in the Gulf below Lake Charles, Louisiana. Tropical storms and hurricanes and the warnings and alerts and conversation that went with them were all part of life on the Texas Gulf Coast, particularly during the September Indianola season. They were another of the "all in a day's work, ma'am" hazards faced by Jack and other bus drivers.

He thought of Dry Fred Bogard, a San Antonio–Corpus driver who had a terrible fear and hate of driving in bad weather. He would call in sick whenever he heard about heavy rain or thunderstorms in an official forecast or felt something coming in his left wrist, which he said was more accurate than most forecasts. The company put up with him until one afternoon he got caught in a surprise Indianola-like crusher of blowing sand and rain on his way north into Pleasanton. He pulled his bus into the driveway next to the café where the buses stopped, jumped out and ran inside, leaving the San Antonio–bound passengers to wonder what was happening. Despite pleas from the woman commission agent who ran the café and several of the passengers, he refused to come back outside and drive on as long as there was even a whiff of sand or a drop of moisture still in the air. He now sold tires and batteries for Kelfer Tire Company in San Antonio.

Jack was no Dry Bogard. His only real concern this afternoon was that it was Friday and the weather was making him late into Victoria. The later he was, the later it would be that he saw Ava.

It was just after he turned on the wipers that he made a decision about her. He was going to ask her her name this afternoon. No matter what else happened, he was going to know her real name by the time he pulled into Corpus Christi this evening.

That was his decision and it would be done. And if that worked, then maybe he would ask her to sit in the Angel Seat. Maybe. That decision was not a sure decision like the one about her name.

My name is Jack, what is yours?

Ava.

Would you care to ride in my Angel Seat, Ava?

I would love to, Jack.

But she wasn't there. She wasn't there!

He looked in the waiting room and then in the coffee shop. She wasn't there. Did this mean she was not coming? Did this mean she was not coming ever again on a Friday afternoon?

Did this mean that it was over between them?

"Our love was not to be," Jacques had said as he lay bleeding to death after being shot by the men who threw Maria off the cliff.

Jack told Johnny Merriweather to give him a first call. He had no choice. He had to go, no matter the weather. The wind was even stronger and the rain was even harder now than when he had pulled in ten minutes earlier. He heard some thunder off in the distance. A flash of lightning came through the waiting-room door.

But he had to go. He was no Dry Fred Bogard.

There was a small canopy under which the passengers could dash in order to keep from getting completely drenched.

Jack and Willie Church used umbrellas to make it even better but it was mostly a lost cause. Everyone, including Jack, got soaked through.

Back inside, counting his tickets, which were also mostly

wet, Jack had to confront the tragedy that lay before him. She was gone. She had stormed into his life like that tail from the Indianola hurricane outside and then blown off out into the sea, never to sit on his bus again. She had wrung out his soul, caused him to forget to throw off papers, run late, pull out an ignition wire and even to think about Loretta dying. How could she do all of that and then sail out of his life? How could she do that to him?

And then, there she was. She came racing through the waiting-room door, her head covered with a newspaper, the rest of her wrapped in a light-pink raincoat.

"Oh, you're still here," she said when she saw Jack.

"Yes, ma'am," he said. "There was no way I would leave without you."

Oh, you're still here.

Yes, ma'am. There was no way I would leave without you.

Jack watched her buy a ticket.

"A one-way to Corpus Christi," she said to Johnny Merri-weather. She put a five-dollar bill down on the counter.

"You bet," said Johnny. He grabbed one of the card tickets out of the ticket dispenser, stamped the back hard with the validator, put it on the counter and said: "Two-twenty out of five."

The water on her face made her even more gorgeous. Jack wished he had a big towel that he could wrap around her and dry her off with. Maybe remove that pink raincoat and what was underneath before doing so. Maybe hold her and then give her a hot bath in a white porcelain bathtub with legs and rub her so she would not catch double pneumonia. Double pneumonia was what his mother had warned him about the most. "Come in here right now, Jack T., before you catch double pneumonia," she used to say. It could be raining or it could be dry, it could be cold or it could be hot, it could be almost anything and she would say it. Jack never understood, for instance, how a tornado warning could give him double pneumonia, but that was his mother's way, so that was it.

Jack knew he was staring. But he could not help it and he did not care. She was just four feet away from him there at the ticket counter.

She took her ticket and her change from the counter and turned to face Jack. But she said nothing.

"Well, it's all aboard for Corpus and the Valley," Jack said. Willie Church was standing there with an umbrella. "Let me hold this over you, ma'am," Willie said.

"Why, thank you so much," she said.

"We don't even know what to call you," Jack said as he followed her and Willie to the door.

Why, thank you so much.

We don't even know what to call you.

She did not answer. She must not have heard him over all the noise and commotion from the rain and the wind.

At the door to the bus, Jack said to her, "Why don't you just take that seat up there across from me?"

She glanced around at him, smiled and said, "That would be nice."

That would be nice.

And there, in a few seconds, she was in his Angel Seat.

Ava was sitting in his Angel Seat!

—

The storm was worse. Maybe the dispatcher in Houston had heard it wrong. Maybe the forecast was for that Indianola to come right down the coast along Highways 59 and 77, right on Jack's tail.

By his watch it was 3:45 in the afternoon but by his sight it was nighttime outside. It was that dark.

Lightning cracked off in the distance ahead. He was just going under the railroad underpass on the western outskirts of Victoria. There was no traffic. Everybody had sense enough to stay off the roads until this thing passed. And it would pass. That was the great and good thing about storms, even Indianolas, down here. They came fast, hit and then they were gone.

Ava's view was the same as his out the front windshield. She was looking at the storm. So was everyone else on the bus. There were eighteen passengers in all, less than half a full load. The weather probably kept away others, people who just decided it was not worth going through all of this to get to Woodsboro or Corpus or Harlingen or wherever. They would put off their trips until tomorrow or another day.

She didn't put off her trip. She came through the early darkness, the sweeping rain, the powerful wind, to ride with him to Corpus.

And now there she sits not more than five feet away from him in his Angel Seat.

He wanted to ask her again about what to call her. He wanted to look at her and to smell her. But there was some serious driving to do first.

Jack slowed his speed to just under fifty miles per hour. Even with the headlights on high beam, he could barely see anything more than fifty yards ahead. He knew the road as well as he knew his own name, but that did not help him see a possible broken-down car or a blown-down tree or pole on the road. A Greyhound driver in Minnesota lost his life and four of his twenty-one passengers last year when he drove right into an electrical power pole that had fallen over the highway. It cracked the front axle right out from under the bus and caused it to flip over on its side and roll down an embankment into a flooded creek bed.

They said the driver was decapitated by a tree limb that came through the windshield right in his face.

Her hair had not gotten that wet. A few strands had come

loose and were down over her forehead, the way Ava Gardner's hair was down across her face when she rode away with a terrible man at the end of *Show Boat*. It only made Ava, his Ava, look more of what she already was. Which was stunningly beautiful.

"This is a real Indianola," he said to her across in the Angel Seat.

He shot his eyes to his right toward her. She nodded but said nothing.

Is it possible she doesn't know what an Indianola is? "Indianolas are what we call the worst storms," he said.

Again, she nodded but said not a word.

Who are you, where do you come from?

I cannot tell you.

Why not?

Because I am a spy for my country.

You are not an American?

I can not say any more.

Please do not say our love is not to be.

I will not say it.

He slowed down as he went through Inairi and then Vidauri. The Indianola was traveling right along with them. It wasn't getting any worse but it was also not getting any better. It was almost as if it was stuck right there on the top of the bus.

The temperature outside was warmer than that inside the bus, which was cool from the air-conditioning. That caused the windshield to fog up badly. The defroster spewed out only hot air, which made him and the bus interior hot, so he kept switching it off and on.

He eased the speed down another couple of miles per hour. He didn't want to have any tree limbs coming through the windshield at him—or her. He did not want to do anything that might cause her harm or discomfort.

Also, the slower he went, the longer he would have with her. Nobody, not even Pharmacy, could question his being late in this weather. A frogman in a submarine would have trouble in this weather was what Paul had said after an earlier Indianola.

A frogman in a submarine. Why can't I talk cleverly like that?

"A frogman in a submarine would have trouble in this weather," he said across to her in the Angel Seat.

He looked around long enough to see her smile. But that was all she did.

Look at that creature of beauty and love and all the rest. She should be in the movies, like the other Ava. She's certainly prettier than the actress who played Maria in that dirty spies thing. Much, much prettier. But she, his Ava, would never play in a movie like that. She was not that kind of woman.

What kind of woman was she?

Was she the kind who would accept and return the love of a bus driver named Jack T. Oliver? A Master Operator named Jack T. Oliver? Was she the kind who would permit a man, any man, to put his hands down the front of her blouse? His hands up the front of her dress? Would she allow a man to kiss her tenderly and passionately upon her breasts?

Would she go to the H.E.B. grocery store with him and throw things into the cart? Does she like to go to the movies? What kinds of movies? Would she do the checkbook every week, the way Loretta does? Jack hated doing the checkbook. What about going to the bathroom? He and Loretta had no problems doing everything in front of each other. But he had heard from some of the drivers that there were women who were too bashful to do it in front of their husbands. One guy's wife insisted on wearing her bra to bed! What about Ava? Does she like peanut butter? Coke or

Pepsi? Or not either one? Dr. Pepper? Does she drink beer? Or whiskey? Can she swim? Does she like to swim? Would she listen to Kern Tipps's Humble Oil broadcasts of the Southwest Conference games on the radio with me? Does she eat meat loaf? Would she make me meat loaf?

There were a lot of things like that to know about somebody . . .

He lost his concentration. He thought he knew where he was but he was not sure.

There was a flash of lightning. Were those people up there on the side of the road? Were they waving at him?

He flashed his lights and goosed the defroster to full power but it was too late. Yes, there were two people! He passed them. They were waving to him, all right, trying to flag him down. My God, why would anybody be standing out in this weather to catch this bus?

Talk about double pneumonia.

He braked the bus to a stop, but he did it slowly and carefully to make sure there would be no sliding on the wet pavement.

He could not see them in the outside rearview mirrors. He had overshot them by a long way. They must be a hundred yards back up there.

He looked around. Yes, he was on that small stretch two miles this side of Refugio. He saw the crossroads ahead there with Farm Road 682. There was no traffic; the shoulder was wide enough to accommodate the bus comfortably.

He threw the gear into reverse. I'll back up awhile and meet those poor people halfway. They must be drenched by now. And if they have any baggage, there is no telling how wet it is.

Rotating his eyes from the left mirror to the right mirror and then back, he started that bus backing down the shoulder.

He went twenty yards maybe but still he could see no people. Where were they? Did they give up? Did they think he had not seen them?

What is that? He got a glimpse of something white on the right. Oh, my God, is it a car?

He jerked the steering wheel to the right and put on the brakes. He felt a bump against the bus back there. Then another. He had hit something. What?

Oh, my God.

It wasn't that hard. It was something soft. A dog? A cow? Right, it was probably another damned calf.

He knew Ava was watching him but there was nothing he could do about that. She would just have to watch. There was nothing to say to her because he did not know what had happened. All he knew was that he had missed seeing some passengers who wanted to ride his bus. And now he was trying his best to make up for what he had done by backing up toward them and keeping them from getting any wetter than they already were.

But he didn't have time to tell Ava all of that. Not now. Not right now.

He yanked up the emergency brake from the floor, grabbed the umbrella and the slicker, hit the door lever and stepped down and out of the bus.

A stream of rain crashed into his face. The sky lit up. Crack! went some thunder off somewhere.

He put his right hand against the side of the bus for balance and bearings and moved toward the rear. The wind was blowing against him. He put his head down.

He felt the motor hatch. He was halfway back. He knew the rear tires were coming up.

Oh, my God, what is that? Something soft. An arm? A leg? He looked down.

It's a person. Lying under the two dual tires. He saw red running from the person. It was a kid! A girl! She was pinned under the tires.

She had been almost cut in two by the bus!

He fell to the ground, to his knees. He saw her face. Her eyes were wide open, staring up at the bottom of that bus.

Dead. This girl was dead!

He stood up and stepped away. There was another streak of lightning.

Somebody else is back there. There's another person back there.

He came around to the rear of the bus. Lying half under the bus and half out was a grown woman. She was also bleeding, particularly from her mouth and ears. The rain was trying to wash it away the second it came but there was too much. There was too much blood.

She was dead. She was dead, too. Both of them were dead. He had run over and killed two people. A grown woman and a girl. Both of them. He had run over and killed them with bus #4107.

He ran with the Indianola wind back to the front of the bus and leaped inside.

"Everything's fine," he said to Ava and the other passengers. "Sorry for the delay. Everything's fine now. We've got a real Indianola on our hands out there. But everything's fine."

He tossed the raincoat onto the floor next to his driver's seat, gunned the engine, threw it in first gear and eased off the shoulder onto the highway for Corpus Christi.

She was looking right at him now. He could feel her eyes on the right side of his face.

"Everything's fine," he said again but did not look at her.

I know it is, Jack.

But they are dead.

It's going to be all right, Jack.

I killed them.

No you didn't, Jack. It was their fault.

I'll call the highway patrol and an ambulance at Refugio.

If you do that, you'll lose everything. They'll take away your gold badge, Jack.

You noticed the badge?

How could I not have noticed that, Jack dear.

———

There, again, was Refugio.

He did not want to stop at Adele Lyman's place. He just wanted to keep moving, to drive right on through town as fast as he could. But there were two people on the bus going to Refugio. They might not like it at all if he did not stop, if he never stopped.

Maybe he would never stop. Not only not at Refugio but also not at Woodsboro or Sinton or Odem or Calallen or even Corpus. Just keep right on to the Valley, to Robstown, or even all the way to Kingsville, or why not stay right on Highway 77 down through the King Ranch to Raymondville and Harlingen and even to Brownsville. Why stop there? Go on over the border to Matamoros, to Mexico.

By the time he got there there might even be a poster at the border station.

WANTED FOR DOUBLE MURDER: Jack T. Oliver, Great Western Trailways Master Operator. Last seen driving ACF-Brill IC-41, bus #4107, into Matamoros with eighteen passengers onboard. One of the passengers was the most beautiful woman in the world, a White Widow who was last seen sitting in the Angel Seat. Oliver is wanted for the brutal killing of two innocent people near the intersection of U.S. Highway 77 and Farm Road 682 east of Refugio, Texas. He ran over them with bus #4107. He is armed with a ticket punch and is wearing a gold badge on his uniform cap and should be considered dangerous to one and all.

Nobody saw what happened, Jack dear. It was raining. Even if somebody was right there they could not have seen it. Relax, Jack dear. Relax. Please relax, Jack dear. Please relax.

You saw it.

No, I didn't.

I saw it.

No you didn't, Jack dear. You saw nothing. You couldn't see anything because of the rain and the wind and it was dark.

"You've never been this late," Adele Lyman said to him when he blew into the door.

"Any express?" His eyes went to the black phone on her desk. He should go to it now, this second, and report the accident to Slick Carlton or someone. Slick Carlton. This storm, almost an Indianola, had probably made for a terrible afternoon for him, maybe even washed the grease right out of his hair.

"Not even one small petal from one small flower," Adele said. "You look awful. What happened?"

He stopped at the door. "What do you mean?"

"You look like you've been run over by something."

"Run over?"

He had always disliked Adele Lyman. Now she scared him. How could she have known what happened? It was a few minutes ago and nobody saw it, nobody knew. Not anybody real.

Not anybody.

"Your raincoat is wet and messed up and so is your cap with that new gold badge. You look like something the cat drug in. And that, Mr. On Time Oliver, is something you don't normally look like anymore."

"This storm is worse than I was ready for, I guess. It's like an Indianola."

The phone. This was the time. Call Slick now or never call, Jack. Call now or never be able to explain to Pharmacy, to Mr. Glisan, to Slick, to Loretta, to the world, why he did not immediately report what had happened. Call now.

Call now.

Hello, highway patrol, this is Jack T. Oliver of Great Western Trailways. There's been an accident and I want to report it to my friend Slick Carlton. I just ran over two people and killed them. They are lying dead on Highway 77, two miles east of Refugio. I am really sorry it happened. Please tell Slick I am really sorry it happened. They were trying to flag me down, I couldn't see them in the storm. Once I did, I was way down the highway so I backed toward them down the shoulder. Something happened and I hit them with my bus. One of them is just a girl. The other is a grown woman. Both of them had black hair. They may both be Tamales. You know, Mexicans. Both of them are bleeding badly. I am so sorry it happened. I have a schedule to keep now. But I did want you to tell Slick Carlton about it.

"I hear it's already clearing over at Sinton," Adele said.

"Good," Jack said. "I'm gone."

I'm gone.

———

Ava had her eyes closed and her head back on the seat headrest when he sat back down behind the steering wheel across the aisle. He looked at her for several long seconds.

Will you go to Mexico with me, Ava dear?

No, no, Jack dearest. Not Mexico. I cannot go to Mexico.

Why not?

Why not is why.

He moved #4107 back onto the highway. The storms were still there, still blowing against the bus, and blowing inside his head.

He saw the face of the dead girl and the dead woman. Now they were completely covered with blood mixed with rain and sand and mud. He saw himself come through the front door of his house in Corpus. He smelled the meat loaf, but no one was there. Loretta was gone. Their wedding picture on the mantel in the living room had a black ribbon around the right side, her side of the picture. Loretta was gone.

He drove #4107 right through Woodsboro without even stopping. It was an accident. He forgot to. Everything was an accident. He didn't even notice until he was on the west side of town, already two miles past the depot at La Hacienda Motor Hotel. Nobody had stood up and said anything, which meant nobody was going to Woodsboro. He remembered from the tickets. Yes, nobody was going to Woodsboro. If there were passengers waiting at the La Hacienda for his bus . . . well, they could catch the next one.

He went into the kitchen and opened the oven. It was cold and there was nothing in it but the smell of meat loaf.

—

The rain had almost stopped and the wind was almost quiet and the sky was almost clear by the time he got to Sinton twenty-four minutes later. Stopped, quiet and clear.

Was it stopped, quiet and clear back there at Highway 77 and Farm Road 682? Had someone come across the bodies of the woman and the girl? How much blood would be left along the side of the road?

How could he ever drive by there again?

How could he drive a bus anywhere again?

There are other things to do with your life, Jack dearest.

I have to be up here behind this wheel.

"You make this trip a lot, I have noticed," he said to her across the aisle.

"That's right," she replied.

He tried to come up with something else to say. Something bright and witty and appropriate. His mind was blank and numb.

His mind was stopped, quiet and clear.

He drove on toward Corpus Christi in silence. There she was in his life, right there next to him and he could not talk to her, he could not break the silence.

—

At Odem, just after he passed Smitty's Seafood Heaven and Earth, he came to his Master Operator, master person senses. Of course he would turn himself in the second he arrived at the Corpus depot. Of course he would tell the dispatcher, who was probably Jennings, to call Slick or somebody at the highway patrol and get on with making amends for what had happened. There was simply no way he could live with what he had done, even if he got away with it. He would wake up every morning, drink every cup of coffee, eat every bite of meat loaf, go to bed every night, go to every movie, go and do everything in his life from now on thinking of that woman and the girl and their blood in the rain. They must have relatives. Were they a daughter and a mother? Where was the father?

You are a better man than this, Jack T. Oliver.

He so much wanted to talk to Ava about it. He so much wanted to say, with real words, what he had in his mind. He wanted her to know what he had done, what he thought about her, what he was now going to do. He so much wanted to say something, anything at all, to his White Widow in the Angel Seat, to his Ava. But his lips would not move.

He looked at her, right at her, when he got off in Sinton and Odem to unload passengers. He remembered to do his job now. He had driven right on through Woodsboro but he would not do that again. He would never do that again. Master Operators do not drive through towns without stopping at bus depots. Jack T. Oliver would never ever do such a thing. He had done it once, just a while ago at Woodsboro, but he would never ever do it again. Not at Sinton, not at Odem, not anywhere.

She, Ava, was not paying any attention to him. She kept her head and eyes slanted always slightly to her right, to see out the right front of the windshield. Her mind was away from him, he was sure, along with her eyes. It was like he was not even there, like this bus was not even being driven by him or by anybody.

Look at me! Look at me, Ava!

Ahead, he saw the early-evening lights of Corpus. It would be the last time he would see them from behind the wheel of a Great Western Trailways Silversides Thruliner. Twelve years and twenty-one days after becoming an intercity bus driver, one week and a day after becoming a Master Operator, he was through. They would fire him for this. They would have to. Pharmacy and Mr. Glisan and the other bosses at Great Western Trailways could not have drivers behind the wheels of their buses who run over people and then keep driving. It simply could not be tolerated.

Look at me! Look at me, Ava!

This would be the last time she would be his passenger. The last time he would take, punch and tear her ticket. The last time he would thank her for riding Great Western Trailways.

The last time he would see her!

Please look at me. Please look at me.

She could not hear him and she did not look at him.

—

"I must see you again," he said.

"What?"

"This cannot end this way."

"What way? What are you talking about?"

He was blocking her exit from the bus. They were at the Corpus Christi bus depot. It was now or never.

She tried to step around him but he moved to prevent it. Other passengers coming down out of the bus had to squeeze around them both. They had to find their way to the ground by themselves, without the help of Jack's hand on an elbow.

"What is your name?" he asked her. "I call you Ava."

"My name? Why do you want to know my name? Did you say Ava? Please. People are waiting for me. I must go."

"What people?"

"Please, Mr. . . . ."

"Oliver. Jack T. Oliver. You have heard my name four times now. Jack T. Oliver. I am Jack T. Oliver. This is the fourth Friday I have driven you here to Corpus. I was off getting my gold badge last Friday or this would have been the fifth."

"Mr. Oliver, please. I do not know what you are talking about. I must go. If you wouldn't mind moving out of my way now."

"I was thinking about you just before it happened."

"What happened? Please, now. Move out of my way. I am already very late."

"My wife just died. Her name was Loretta."

"I am very sorry. Please, now. Let me by."

He moved out of the way. And then watched her, as he had three previous times, walk down Schatzel Street and out of his life.

No. He could not give her up. Not now. Not yet.

Nobody had seen what happened at Highway 77 and Farm Road 682. Why should he throw away the badge, the job and the woman he loved all because of an accident? It was simply a terrible accident. Telling what happened would not bring those two poor people back to life.

—

"It must have been hell out there where you just came from," said Sweet Jennings, the dispatcher. They called him Sweet because he wasn't. If he had his way, buses would be still unairconditioned and unheated, drivers and ticket agents would work for nothing, loud children and preachers traveling on buses would be against the law.

"It was so bad around Refugio I could barely see," Jack said.

"You do realize you came in here just now forty-two minutes late?"

"I didn't realize it was that bad."

"Call for anything over thirty minutes. You know the rules."

"Sorry. I got distracted by the storm, I guess."

"Bay City's underwater."

"Any other reports?"

"No. Except for Galveston. I heard a Texas Red Rocket Flxible got knocked loose from the High Island Ferry. Nobody hurt but a lot of people got wet."

"Me, too."

"You look it."

"Thanks."

—

The smell of meat loaf hit him the moment he stepped inside the house. At first he thought he must be imagining it. Then he heard a woman's voice say, "Jack? Is that you?"

He did not answer.

"I was worried sick that you got lost in that Indianola."

Loretta came through the kitchen door toward him. He had never been so happy and so sad at the same time in his life.

"You look a mess," she said, grabbing him and hugging him to her. "Let's get you out of that wet uniform and into a hot bath."

Loretta was not dead. It was the woman and the girl who were dead back on the highway near Refugio.

"I thought God was punishing me for what I was thinking about you, Jack, and what I had said to you, Jack. I really did think that was it. God was punishing me by making you die and disappear in an Indianola."

It had never occurred to Jack that God had anything to do with anything that had happened, was happening or ever would happen to him.

CHAPTER 10

*I*t was almost one o'clock in the morning but Jack was not asleep. He had faked sleep so Loretta would finally quit asking him what was wrong besides his having been in an awful storm, almost an Indianola. So he was sitting in the kitchen when the phone rang. He picked it up before the first ring finished.

"Jack, is that you?" It was Slick Carlton of the Texas highway patrol.

"Yeah, Slick," Jack said.

"Sorry to call you at home and so late but you know about duty and work and all of that."

Jack said he knew about that.

"We've got two hit-and-run victims up on Seventy-seven, one point three miles east of Refugio, Jack. We can't tell much about them except that they were hit and run over by something, somebody. Adele Lyman, our friend the fool, said you were through there about then. Did you see anything that might help us figure out what happened?"

"Not a thing, Slick. Not one thing."

"We can't tell much when it might have happened because of the storm. That was a doosey wasn't it?"

"Sure was."

"Several times I thought I was going to be blown right off the road. I told you an Indianola might get me someday."

"But it didn't."

"Yeah, right. I was lucky this time. The victims were a mother and her daughter. According to what the mother had on her, they were from Fort Worth. She had a driver's license and she had a wad of money. I can't imagine what somebody from Fort Worth would be doing out in the middle of the storm like that with a wad of money."

"Me neither."

"Well, sorry again to call so late. Thought it was worth a try. You know the names of any of the passengers who were with you?"

"No."

"Too bad. There's always a chance one of them might have seen something you didn't. Go back to sleep."

"Will do, Slick."

"I'm not feeling so slick right now, Jack, I can tell you that. I got rainwater up my nose and in my ears and between my toes and up and between every other single part of me. If somebody squeezed me like a sponge I could produce enough water to fill a goodly-sized lake."

"Yeah."

—

Then just after two o'clock that afternoon Sweet Jennings called from the dispatcher's office. Loretta was at work because one of her weekend ad takers quit and another was down with a bad cold. Jack was in the bathroom fooling with the bathtub faucets. Both were leaking and he was hoping all that was needed was new washers.

"Mr. Glisan called from Houston just now," Sweet said to Jack. "He said he and Pharmacy were about to get in a car to drive to Corpus. They want to see you when they get here. Should be tonight about seven or eight."

"Tonight? They want to see me tonight?"

"That's what he said."

"What about?"

"That's what I asked. 'What about?' He wouldn't say. He talked like you would know, though. Guess not, huh? That figures."

—

Jack went back to the bathtub. The washer on the hot-water faucet had melted almost away. He started scraping off its remains.

Mr. Glisan and Pharmacy do not get into a car on a Saturday afternoon to drive to Corpus unless it is important and serious. Obviously it has to do with the two dead Tamales. He hated himself for thinking of them as Tamales. And colored people as Blues. He hated Adele Lyman for doing that to him, although it was probably better than calling them wetbacks and niggers like everybody else did.

What do Pharmacy and Mr. Glisan know? How could they know what happened? They don't know what happened? If they didn't know what happened why would they jump in a car on a Saturday afternoon and drive five hours or more to talk to him? Could there have been somebody off in the field watching the whole thing? Could the dead woman's husband, the dead girl's father, have been watching? No?

Not him, not anyone? They would have come running out to see about it all?

What were two people from Fort Worth doing out there on that highway in that storm? They must have been driving a car and it broke down. Or got washed out in the storm. Sure. That is what happened. Why didn't Slick Carlton and his people think of that? Obviously, that is what happened. The Tamale woman and her daughter were driving from Fort Worth to Corpus and the storm got in the way and caused them to stop. So here comes a bus, let's flag it down. Thank God, one of them probably said. Here comes a bus!

Here comes a bus.

Pharmacy and Mr. Glisan could be coming about something else.

Don't be stupid, Jack. What else could it be?

Woodsboro. The Woodsboro agent could have reported him for not stopping. Yes, that is it!

Oh, come on, Jack. Would the head of operators and the division superintendent drive all the way from Houston to Corpus to chew out a driver who missed a stop in a storm, almost an Indianola?

I guess not.

—

He told Loretta he had to go to the depot to finish some paperwork from the Friday storm. A tree limb on the road near El Campo had punctured a tire, he said. There were some questions about it, he said.

It was clear to Jack that Loretta did not believe him. It was clear she thought he was going out to meet his girlfriend, whoever and wherever she was. For reasons he could not understand, she was very peaceful about it at first. Maybe thinking he had died in the storm had changed her. Whatever,

146 | JIM LEHRER

she was peaceful about his leaving the house this Saturday
night, something he had seldom done except to drive a run.

Her peacefulness ended at the front door. "What's her
name, Jack?" she said in a voice full of war.

"Ava Gardner," he replied.

"That's not funny, Jack." Loretta was not a violent person
but he knew that if she had been, he would have been hit
over the head with a lamp or a skillet or a hatchet or some
other heavy or sharp object.

—

He drove the Dodge first to the Tarpon Inn. He didn't want a
beer or some peanuts or anything in particular. His only
thought was about College. Maybe he would be there;
maybe he really was smarter than every other bus driver.
Maybe they would have something to say to each other that
would matter. Something that would help. Maybe he could
be his Kenny of Kingsville.

College was there, all right. So was Senator, the local drivers' union president, and Jack walked into the middle of a
discussion at the bar about politics, the single most boring
subject there was to Jack. Put Senator with Willow and a few
drunk bus drivers and shrimpers and words flew. It took a
few minutes for Jack to catch up to the fact that somebody,
probably Willow, had started naming names of people at the
Corpus Christi city hall, the state capitol in Austin, as well as
with President Eisenhower and the Congress in Washington,
who were Reds. Senator was hot.

"You are slandering good people, that is what you are
doing," he was saying when Jack took his place on a stool
next to College, who seemed, as usual, to be listening but not
participating, because all of these people were beneath him in
some other world.

"They're out to take over the schools and the water," said a guy at the bar Jack did not recognize.

"That is absolute grease-monkey shit!" screamed Senator.

"That's not what I heard on the radio!" Willow screamed back.

"The people on the radio wouldn't know grease-monkey shit if they stepped in a barrel of it," said Senator.

"They know a lot more than some damned stupid bus driver!"

Jack motioned at College to join him somewhere else. Jack took his Lone Star and went over to a table in a corner as far away from the bar as he could get. And in a minute or two, College, his beer in hand, sat down across from him.

"I'm not even sure I know what a Red is," Jack said to College.

"That makes you even with every one of those people yelling about them over there," said College. He made no effort to hide his disgust.

"What are they?"

"What?"

"Reds . . . Communists."

College, for the second time in Jack's presence, smiled. "They are people who think people like you should run things."

"Bus drivers?"

"Yep. And carpenters and plumbers and salesclerks and ditchdiggers and steelworkers and roughnecks."

"I can barely run a bus."

"I thought you were one of our elite."

"Our what?"

"Our best." And College smiled again, but this time Jack realized there was no difference between his smile and his frown. They both expressed disgust.

"You ever been in serious trouble before, College?" Jack asked.

"None of your business, Jack."

"I'm not prying."

"You're prying."

"I think I'm in trouble and I want to talk about it."

"Not to me, Jack. Not to me." College grabbed his bottle of beer and stood up. "I can't help you."

"You're smarter than me."

College leaned down right into Jack's face. "If I was smarter than you, then I wouldn't be driving a bus with you and Sunshine and all the rest."

He straightened up and headed back to the bar.

Clearly Jack had not found his Kenny of Kingsville.

"Sunshine?" Jacked yelled after College. "What about him?"

"I hear he's in trouble, too."

———

Jack arrived at the bus depot just after seven. Mr. Glisan and Pharmacy were already there, sitting in the district passenger agent's empty office upstairs. They were waiting for him.

"You-all made good time," Jack said when he walked in.

"Pharmacy did the driving," Mr. Glisan said. "As they say, he never met a floorboard he didn't like."

Mr. Glisan was behind the small desk in the room. Pharmacy pulled up two wooden chairs for him and Jack. The chairs were brown and looked like they had come from a drugstore. A Rexall pharmacy? The Corpus DPA was named Bill Tillman. His job was to keep the commissioned agents happy and serviced with tickets, express waybills, posters, tariffs and small porcelain bus depot signs to hang outside. There were stacks and boxes and envelopes of all of these kinds of things all over the office. It was a messy place. Tillman had started as a Dallas–San Angelo driver many years ago.

What if I became a DPA, Ava dear? Would you tell me your name and love me then?

We'll just have to see, Jack dear.

It was clear from the second he walked in what Mr. Glisan and Pharmacy had come to talk about.

"There's a problem, Jack," Mr. Glisan said. "We've come to talk to you about a problem."

"Have you got an idea of what it might be?" Pharmacy asked. "Any idea at all?"

"No," Jack said. "Not at all. None."

"We lost two checkers last night outside Refugio," Glisan said.

"Checkers?"

"They were contract employees of Schoellkopf-Greene, a detective agency out of Fort Worth. We hired them."

The faces of those two people came again to Jack. That woman and that girl were checkers? He thought he might not be able to breathe.

"What's wrong there, fella?" Pharmacy asked. "You look kind of strange. Or are you sick?"

"I'm fine," Jack said. What had he done or shown on his face to make Pharmacy say that? "What do you mean you lost 'em?"

"They're dead, Jack. That's really losing 'em, wouldn't you agree?"

Jack said he would so agree.

Mr. Glisan said: "It happened during that storm yesterday afternoon. They were put out there to hop your schedule to Corpus and then come back on the five-thirty. They were found dead along the side of the highway last night. The highway patrol said there were tire marks all over one of them."

"Heavy tire marks," Pharmacy said. "From a truck or maybe even a bus. The rain washed most of it away, so they can't tell for sure."

"Did the highway patrol call you, Jack?" asked Mr. Glisan. "They said they were going to."

"Yes, sir. They called me."

"What in the hell did you tell them?" Pharmacy said.

Mr. Glisan and Rex Al Barney were famous in the company for their one-two. Pop, goes Glisan, pow, goes Pharmacy. Take that, Operator Smith. Take that, Operator Jones.

"I told them I didn't see a thing. I could barely see the highway, if the truth was known."

"The truth is what this is all about, Jack."

Take that, Master Operator Jack T. Oliver.

"Yes, sir."

"Did you see them out there on the highway, Jack?" Mr. Glisan asked. He said it quietly, as if he were asking directions to the First State Bank of Wharton.

"No, sir," Jack said, just as quietly.

"Dead or alive," Pharmacy said. "Never mind what you might have told the highway patrol, did you see them, dead or alive?"

"No, I did not."

"They would have been trying to wave you down," Glisan said.

"There was nobody out on the highway in the kind of weather we had out there yesterday. It was about as close to being an Indianola as it gets without being one, you know."

"I know, I know. It must have been hard to see," said Pharmacy.

"It was."

Glisan said, "Looking at your trip report, Jack, it would seem as if you came by where these two people died at about five-ten or so. You were running late into and out of Victoria but you lost a lot more time after that."

"Fridays. You'd already been having a problem with Fridays," Pharmacy said.

"Nobody could have driven a schedule on time in that yesterday," Jack said.

Glisan again: "They must have died just about the time you drove by. The highway patrol figures it happened between five and five-thirty. Are you sure you didn't see anybody out there trying to flag you down?"

"I am sure."

Now Pharmacy with the pow: "This is the time, the exact moment, to tell the truth, Jack."

"Why would I lie about something like this? If I saw two people trying to flag me down, I would have stopped and picked them up. If they were already dead when I came by, then I probably wouldn't have been able to see them lying alongside the road because of the storm."

"Dead people don't flag down buses, you are sure enough right about that." Pharmacy scooted his chair right up to Jack's. He leaned his big body and face over at Jack just like College had done at the Tarpon Inn. "Did you run down those two people, Jack?"

"No."

"Did you kill those two people, Jack?"

"No."

"What's gone wrong with your Fridays, Jack?"

"Nothing. A string of bad luck or something. I am not in charge of storms. Somebody else like God or Jesus is in charge of storms."

"You are in charge of your bus, Jack. We pinned a gold

badge on you the other night that said to everybody you were the best we have in charge of our buses. The best we have do not run over and kill people and then lie about it."

"Why would I do that?"

"Run over people or lie about it?"

"Both."

"You run over people maybe by accident, you lie about it because you don't want to lose your job, your ass and go to jail."

Jack T. Oliver, Master Operator, felt nausea in his throat. But he also felt good about himself. He had, until this point at least, done very well for himself. He had stood his ground against Pop and Pow, Pow and Pop. He had not given in. He had not split or cracked or broken.

They were checkers! That woman and the girl were checkers!

Mr. Glisan, looking down in front of him at a folder on the desk, said: "Let me tell you about the two people who died, Jack. Anna Phyllis Fontes, age forty-two, a former probation officer in Fort Worth. Her husband, José Felix Fontes, is a sergeant in the Fort Worth Police Department. They have five children. One of them, Marguerite Susannah Fontes, age fourteen, was the other victim yesterday. She was a student at Birdville High School outside Fort Worth. She wanted to be a police officer like her father."

"Now she'll never be anything," said Pharmacy, still sitting up close to Jack.

"What were they doing with a fourteen-year-old girl out there as a checker?" Jack asked. It was a reflex kind of question.

"They're smart, these detective outfits," Pharmacy said. "They know that our bus drivers are smart sunsbitches and they know that they have to be smarter. Who in the world, what bus driver in the world, what Master Operator in the world, would ever suspect that a Mexican woman and her teenage daughter flagging down a bus in a storm outside Refugio would be company checkers? Who, Jack, who?"

"Not me, that is for sure."

"How did it happen, Jack?" Mr. Glisan asked. "How did you run over them, Jack? I am sure it was an accident. Tell us about it now before it is too late."

Jack fixed his eye on a small Great Western Trailways bus depot sign that was leaning against the wall in front of him. The sign was beginning to rust away around the two holes where it had been hung. Where had it been hanging? How long had it been there?

Pharmacy said: "It may already be too late, Jack. Vehicular homicide, two counts. Leaving the scene of an accident, one count. You could get fifteen years, Jack. Fifteen years behind bars at Huntsville. You ever been through the penitentiary up there in Huntsville, Jack?"

Jack T. Oliver, Master Operator, shook his head slowly from right to left twice and then stood up.

"I told you I did not do anything," he said. "I am the best bus driver you have or ever will have, except maybe for Paul Madison. You should not have been wasting your time and insulting me by putting checkers on me in the first place . . ."

"We put 'em on everybody, you know that," Mr. Glisan said. "Nobody is above or below temptation. Nobody, and that means you and everybody."

"That's a stupid attitude to have," Jack said. It made him proud of himself again.

"Only stupid people call people smarter than them stupid," Pharmacy said.

"I didn't call you and Mr. Glisan stupid. I called your attitude stupid. You give a guy like me a gold badge and tell me how I am the backbone and the tailbone of the company . . ."

Pharmacy stood, grabbed his chair and threw it across the office. "Shut up, Jack!" he yelled.

Jack jumped, out of fear.

"You killed those people!"

"I told you I did not and I told you I did not and now I am going home."

He took two steps toward the door.

Mr. Glisan said: "You should know something else, Jack. Something that should keep you thinking as you walk out of here now and go home. There was a third person involved in that check. It was a guy with a movie camera operating from a tripod under a piece of canvas he was using as a kind of tent to keep his camera dry. He says you drove right on past the two females who were trying to flag you down and he figured in the storm you didn't see them. He says he was about to run out of film so he headed back to the car, which they had parked down Farm Road 682, for another roll. When he came back the two females were lying there dead. He didn't see anything but he does remember hearing the sound of an engine from back on the highway. It was a heavy-duty engine of some kind. He said he didn't hear much of anything else because of the noise of the rain and thunder and the wind."

"I have already said what I have said," said Jack. "That guy proves I didn't stop. I didn't see them. It was hell seeing anything out there yesterday. I told you that."

Glisan said, in a voice Jack could barely hear, "Fortunately, the other agent left his movie camera running. So we probably will have pictures of everything that happened. They're being processed now. We should have them to look at on Monday."

"Maybe you could join us for a viewing, Jack?" Pharmacy said.

"You are suspended pending our seeing those movies," Mr. Glisan said.

"Suspended?"

"You do not drive a bus again for us until we tell you to. You do not wear the uniform or that new gold badge of Great Western Trailways again until we tell you to."

Jack opened the door to leave.

"One more thing, Jack," Pharmacy said. "That breakdown of yours a week ago Friday. The mechanics here wrote on their report that it looked to them like somebody intentionally screwed up that ignition wire. Who would do something like that?"

"I have no idea," said Jack.

"I have one more thing, too," Mr. Glisan said. "We're going to be trying to locate some of the passengers from your run yesterday. We're hoping they might have seen something you didn't see. The highway patrol asked us to do it. Do you know any of their names right off the top of your head?"

"No."

"Too bad. We'll check the commission agents along the route."

Jack left.

At the bottom of the stairs he came upon Sunshine Ashley. He was sitting in a chair in civilian clothes, looking sadder and droopier than Jack could ever remember.

Sunshine saw Jack and stood up.

"What did they get you for, Jack?" Sunshine said.

"Nothing really," Jack lied. "What about you?"

"They said they had a movie they wanted me to see."

"Well, good luck, Sunshine."

Sunshine said, "I told you they would get us all and they did."

—

He told Loretta nothing of his meeting with Mr. Glisan and Pharmacy. He told her nothing of anything, except that he was going to Padre Island alone the next morning, Sunday morning, instead of driving his regular run east to Houston.

"What's going on, Jack?" she asked, quietly but with violence in between the words.

"I've been suspended."

"Suspended? Why?"

"There was an accident the other night on Highway Seventy-seven and they want me to hang around for the investigation."

"I want to go to Padre with you."

"I need to be by myself."

"Tell me about her, Jack, you bastard."

"I don't know anything about her to tell," Jack said. It was an honest answer, one that clearly made Loretta even angrier because it made no sense.

It made no sense to Jack either.

But what was he going to say? How could he tell the real story to Loretta, his wife, a woman who had done nothing to him except love him, feed him and care for him? How could he say: Yes, it is a woman that has come between us, ruined my life and your life and our lives together. But all I know about her is that she is the most beautiful woman I have ever seen, and she's been riding my bus from Victoria to Corpus on Friday afternoons. I do not know where she lives or what she does when she's not on my bus. I do not even know her name. Yes, I have touched every part of her magnificent body. I have done things with her and to her that I did not even know were there to do until she came into my life. But I have done all of that in my head, only in my mind, my imagination. The only parts of her body I have really touched are her elbows.

"Don't come back in this house with her smell on you, Jack T. Oliver!"

Those were Loretta's parting words to him. They were accompanied by the sound of the front door slamming.

Jack knew what this woman, this Ava, smelled like. That was one thing he did not have to imagine. She smelled like she had just stepped out of a white porcelain bathtub with legs at the four corners.

He was in the garage on the way to the car. As always, he had to step around Oscar, his favorite Santa Claus. It always made him smile to see him. Everybody in the neighborhood said their Christmas decorating was the best in the neighborhood, if not in that whole part of town. Oscar, whose eyes and nose lit up, was four feet tall. He went on the front lawn on one side of the house, the full-sized manger set with life-sized replicas of baby Jesus, Mary and Joseph and the three Wise Men went on the other. Eight strings of red, green, blue and white lights were hung around the windows on the house behind them. White plastic wreaths with red lights in the center went on every window. Jack had picked up Oscar free from a passenger in El Campo who was helping close down a dry-goods store. He told Jack about the Santa they were going to throw away and on an impulse Jack told the guy he wanted it. On the next run-through the Santa was there at the bus depot, Jack loaded it in the baggage compartment and brought it home. He named him Oscar after a high school shop teacher in Beeville he had always liked.

Jack wondered if Ava would be as interested in decorating a house and yard for Christmas.

And he wondered if they would let him do any of it at the Huntsville prison or wherever he was going to end up.

He got in the car, a seven-year-old Dodge two-door, and headed for the beach, for Padre Island.

Padre Island was his paradise. It was the place Jack had been going to since high school to play and to think and to imagine who he was.

———

The *Caller* and everybody else kept talking about the development boom that was coming to Padre. Maybe so, but right now it was still a fifty-mile-long strip of isolated sand that followed the coastline from Corpus down to Brownsville, the Rio Grande Valley and the Mexican border. It was only two miles wide, and except right around Corpus on the north and Brownsville and Port Isabel on the south, where there were Holiday Inns and a handful of stores and houses, it was mostly desolate and unapproachable, except from the sea or by four-wheel-drive Jeeps left over from the military.

There was plenty of room for everybody who wanted to come and walk or ride or fish or do nothing but be on the beach. Nothing but be on the beach was what Jack had come to do.

He drove south on the beach road for the three miles until it petered out; then he parked and started walking south. He was wearing a pair of jeans, a pullover short-sleeved shirt and a pair of high-top white tennis shoes. After a few minutes he took off the shoes. It wouldn't be long now. He came upon two middle-aged men tending fishing poles and then a young man and a young woman lying on a blanket.

He moved off the rough path through the sand and went closer to the water. Oh, my, how he loved this. There was nothing more white and more bright than a spring afternoon like this. The sun bounced off the water and the white sand to make everything white and bright. Even a dark black suit would have been turned white and bright.

A dark black mood would have been turned white and bright.

Jack sat down on the sand. And then he lay down and stretched out, his arms high above his head, his legs as far down as they would go. Here I am, sun. All of me. Here I am, Jack T. Oliver, back for some whiteness and brightness.

He could not count the number of times in his life he had come to Padre and stretched out in the sand like this. He came first with his parents and then with his junior high and high school classmates and finally with Loretta and some older friends.

In the early days he ran as fast as he could into the waves and then wore himself out playing jump-the-waves. And he built forts and houses out of sand. His favorite thing to do was to lie down on the sand as the tide was coming in and stay there as the water came closer and closer, first to his feet and then over his legs and eventually over his face and head.

In high school, he swam in the Gulf and drank beer on the beach. Some of his friends came with their girlfriends to make out, but Jack didn't have a girlfriend in high school. But from about the age of eleven on, he had many sexual experiences on this beach, with cheerleaders and drum majors and English teachers and carhops and theater ushers. All in his head, of course.

When the time did eventually come for Loretta and him to do it for real, it was to Padre he brought her.

It was on this sand that he first put his tongue inside her mouth, he first put his hand on her breasts, on her thighs and on the inside of her legs.

But mostly he came here to be by himself. He was a thinker even if he wasn't a man of great ideas and heavy thoughts, even if he was stupid, even if he was a bus driver. He used his mind to go places and do things. His mother was the only one who really knew he did that a lot, and she said he should be careful with all of that imagining because it could lead him to real trouble someday.

It was on this beach that he thought it all through to realize once and for all that he wanted to drive a bus forever and never go back to Beeville like his mom wanted him to. Jack had just met Loretta and was driving for Nueces Transportation when his mother called him out of the blue. She asked him to come home. Jack told her about the thrill he got from driving a bus and said, who knows, someday he might even move on to intercity, to the big over-the-road buses. She said she was sure that would be great. But weren't there buses in Beeville he could drive? No, he said, there weren't any buses in Beeville. Only school buses, and he didn't want to drive school buses. She said Dr. EyeBob had truly accepted the fact that his son was not going to be an eye doctor who specialized in the new things called contact lenses. But it didn't matter that much anymore and he wanted his only son back in Beeville. Come home and live your life with us, Jack, said Mrs. Dr. EyeBob. Jack listened to what she said and went out to Padre, lay down on the beach and thought it through to deciding he really did want to be a bus driver.

Now that would soon be over too. He would no longer be a bus driver. What would he be? Jack T. Oliver, child and woman killer. Jack T. Oliver, hit-and-run driver. Jack T. Oliver, sex maniac.

Jack T. Oliver, ex-convict.

Jack T. Oliver, ex-son.

He dug his heels deeper into the sand. He stuck the fingers of both hands down into the sand. He banged his head against the sand several times. He moved his butt back and forth to burrow out a deeper hole. He did the same with his shoulders and legs.

Into the sand. He wanted to go deeper and deeper into the sand, his sand. He wanted to disappear. Where is the water? Where are the waves? Cover me up, water.

Cover me up.

He closed his eyes. He tried to imagine the movie the company had of his killing that woman and her daughter. Black and white. It had to be in black and white. Color was for Kathryn Grayson and Howard Keel, Judy Garland and Fred Astaire, Donald O'Connor and Vera Ellen. Black and white was for a woman-obsessed bus driver backing his ACF-Brill IC-41, bus #4107, over helpless Tamale women and children.

He saw the bus hit the girl. She fell down and the right rear tires rolled on top of her, right in her middle. The woman, screaming, ran to her and was hit by the bus and knocked back. Her head hit the concrete. Everything was wet and then red.

He opened his eyes. What he saw was bright and white and blue. Here came a cloud from the right. It was a bright and white cloud that would do no harm to the sky or to any person or thing.

He tried again to dig himself deeper into the sand. But it was no use. He could go no farther.

CHAPTER 11

*T*hey told him to come to a room at the Hotel Surf rather than to the bus depot. The Surf was a clean second-level hotel on Corpus Christi beach on the other side of the port. The main hotels were on the west side, the downtown side.

There was a third man in the room with Mr. Glisan and Pharmacy. Jack caught the name as Peck. Mr. Peck of Schoellkopf-Greene Detective Agency Inc. He was short, trim and dressed in a dark brown suit like a cop.

The room was larger than a standard Hotel Milam room. It had two large double beds plus a sitting area with a couch and two or three chairs around a table. There was a movie projector on the table and a portable movie screen unrolled and ready against a far wall.

"Want to see our little movie, Jack?" Mr. Glisan asked after they all sat down.

It was a question Jack had not come prepared to answer.

He had assumed he had to watch the movie. He assumed he had no choice. He assumed it was part of the punishment, the sentence, the end.

"No," he said. "Not if I don't have to."

"I don't blame you," Pharmacy said. "It is sickening. I mean sickening. To watch those two helpless people go to their deaths, their bodies crushed, that blood flowing out of them and all over that highway . . ."

"Forget it, Rex," Mr. Glisan said. Mr. Glisan was one of the few people in the world of Great Western Trailways who ever called Pharmacy by his right first name. Jack wondered what Pharmacy's wife and kids called him. He knew he had a wife and three children because the April issue of the company's employee magazine, *The Thruliner,* had a story about them. The thing Jack remembered most was that Pharmacy's oldest son was an Aggie, a mechanical engineering student at Texas A&M in College Station. Whenever Jack had thought about going to a four-year college, which had not been very often, he saw himself as an Aggie. They had an ROTC cadet corps that required every student to wear an army uniform with leather boots that went up the leg to the knee, and according to the teachers at Beeville High, tuition and other expenses at Texas A&M were cheaper than at any other big-time college in Texas.

Mr. Glisan, the Mr. Calm, was clearly in charge of this meeting. Pharmacy was clearly hot-red angry at Jack for what he had done. Mr. Peck showed nothing.

"Do you have anything to say for yourself, Jack, before we go any further?" Mr. Glisan asked.

"About what?"

Pharmacy answered, "About why you violated every rule of the road and this company by backing down an open highway in a rain storm! How you left the scene of an accident in violation of every human and legal law of this state, this land and this company! You left those people dead, lying there along the road. Don't you dare say, 'About what?' "

Jack had spent some time on the sand trying to work out what to say at this moment, this moment that he knew was sure to come. Nothing he thought about saying seemed right, now that it had come time to say it. So he said, "Okay."

"What happened, Jack?" Mr. Glisan said, lowering his voice and the temperature. Mr. Nice Guy.

"If you saw the movie you know what happened," Jack said. He said it quietly and politely, the way he had always said most things to most people.

"I mean in your mind. What happened that caused you to violate your training? You were one of our best. What happened to you to cause you to do what you did?"

"I don't have anything to say about my mind."

"You have money troubles?"

"No, sir."

"No outstanding debts on your mind?"

"No, sir."

"Personal problems at home?"

"No, sir."

"Your marriage all right?"

"It's fine."

"You don't have children, do you?"

"No, sir."

"Is that the problem?"

"No, sir."

Pharmacy took over.

"Look, Jack, good men don't suddenly go wrong. Not just like that, not the way you did. With Sunshine, it was different. He couldn't keep his pants on, a common problem among men and bus drivers. But you? There has to be a reason, and we want to know what it is."

Jack looked right at Pharmacy and said, "Why?"

"So, well, you know, so we'll know what to look for in hiring people."

"So you'll never end up with another me?"

"Something like that."

Jack jerked his head back toward Mr. Glisan and said nothing. There would not have been any point in saying what he wanted to say, what was running coherently and precisely through his mind almost to his mouth and lips. Something along the lines of: Only Paul Madison is better than me and that is only because he's been there longer. It is impossible to drive a bus better than I can. One mistake does not change that simple fact. What did Sunshine do? Where did he take off his pants?

"Does it have anything to do with Fridays?" Pharmacy asked.

Jack had decided he would not tell Mr. Glisan, Pharmacy, the police or anyone else about Ava. He might have told College if he had turned out to be his Kenny of Kingsville. He might have told him that this White Widow in his Angel Seat was the reason he lost his concentration and his head that night in the storm. But she was no excuse. Nothing like that could ever be an excuse for a Master Operator, the best bus driver in the system except for Paul Madison.

"Nothing at all," Jack said to Pharmacy. "As I told you in Houston, I had some bad luck a few Fridays in a row."

"That made late the man who is never late."

Jack decided to get this thing over with. "Pharmacy, listen. I know what's coming to me so let's get on with it."

"What do you think is coming to you?" Mr. Glisan asked.

"I'm going to be fired, I am going to be charged and tried and probably sent to jail."

"Why are you so goddamn calm about it?" Pharmacy shouted.

"Because I have already run it all through my mind. I lay out on the sand at Padre all afternoon thinking about it. I saw myself trying to get a job back at Nueces Transportation or selling bait over at Ingleside. I saw myself standing before a judge with a mustache and a long nose who was sending me to Huntsville for ninety-nine years. I saw myself wearing a prison uniform and eating in a big prison cafeteria and walking around a big exercise yard, like in the movies. I know what's coming. I have seen it all already. So please, let's get on with it."

"Nobody can imagine everything that happens before it happens," Pharmacy said.

"Nobody but me, I guess."

Both Pharmacy and Mr. Glisan turned toward Mr. Peck, who up to this moment had not said anything except hello.

"Are you willing to sign a statement, confessing to what you did?" he asked.

That was something Jack had not thought about on the beach at Padre. So he said, "No."

"Why not?"

"I don't know. What's the point? You have the movie."

"What if we didn't have the movie?"

Peck was a smooth talker. It reminded Jack of the eleventh grade in Beeville when everyone was required to choose a magazine article and make a speech to the class about it. He did his on a reformed embezzler who had come out of prison and helped invent Scotch tape someplace up north, like Minnesota. When Jack opened his mouth to speak, his voice cracked into many pieces and went higher than most girls'. And this caused his legs to shake, like his left one had the first afternoon Ava came aboard his bus. Think of a flannel shirt, the teacher had said. Think about talking like a flannel shirt feels—soft and smooth and soothing. Mr. Peck talked like he was thinking of a flannel shirt.

"You do, so why ask?"

Mr. Peck looked again at Pharmacy and Mr. Glisan, and Jack saw something pass among them that made him think they might not have the movie after all. "I've changed my mind," he said.

"About what?" Pharmacy said.

"I want to see the movie."

Mr. Peck did not look again at the other two men in the room. Instead, he reached inside a large white envelope and pulled out a black-and-white photograph. He handed it to Jack.

"Do you know this woman?"

Jack took the photo of Ava, his White Widow in the Angel Seat, in both hands. It was a photograph of her from the chest up. She had on a blouse that was light-colored and short-sleeved. Her eyes were open and she was smiling. He wanted to pull her to him and hold her tight against his chest. Nausea raced through him, and he started to sweat. He tried to think about flannel. If he had been standing, there was no telling what would have been happening to his legs and his every other part.

"So you know her all right," said Mr. Peck, who could not have helped but notice what was happening to Jack.

"I don't know her name," Jack mumbled. "I don't even know her name."

"The highway patrol found her," said Mr. Peck. "She told them she was on your bus Friday afternoon during the storm. She was in the Angel Seat. She told them what happened."

Jack, still staring at the photograph, did not respond.

"She has given them a full statement," Mr. Peck said.

Jack heard that and he thought about that. And he said, "What did she say happened?"

"You know, the whole story," Mr. Peck said.

"What did she say the full story was?"

"Nobody knows that better than you do, Jack, goddamn it," Pharmacy said.

Mr. Peck and the other two, Jack concluded, had absolutely nothing. No movie, no eyewitness account. The White Widow in the Angel Seat had nothing to tell anybody except that he stopped the bus, got out and came back a few minutes later and drove away. She could not have seen the dead woman and her daughter or anything behind the bus. Nobody on that bus could have, but she in particular could not have, from the Angel Seat up front.

"What did she say she saw?" Jack asked, looking right at Mr. Peck.

"I can't tell you that. It would be in violation of investigative procedures."

"What is her name?"

"I can't tell you that."

"Who is she besides her name?" Mr. Peck asked.

"I don't know. Just a bus passenger."

Just a bus passenger.

Jack felt fine again. He said to Mr. Peck, "Is showing me the movie also a violation of your investigative procedures?"

Mr. Peck's facial expression, which was all business, did not change. He was obviously used to getting people to confess to things.

Jack was beginning to decide that he, Jack T. Oliver, was not as stupid as Mr. Peck and a lot of other people, including College, thought he was—and even he himself had thought he was.

He decided then and there that he would not say another word. Not one word. If anything else was said in that room at the Hotel Surf about what had happened involving bus #4107 1.3 miles east of Refugio in the middle of that Friday storm, which was almost an Indianola, it was not going to be said by Jack T. Oliver.

So that left the talking to the other three men. They had a lot to say about why they would love to make a deal with Jack. A deal that gave them what they wanted, which was silence and no trouble, in exchange for what they figured Jack wanted, which was to walk out of the Hotel Surf free and clear.

Free and clear to do what? To be what? To go where?

—

Progress Paul Madison was sitting in the center of the center section of the theater, about halfway between the rear and the screen. The usher said that was where he always sat. He was one of only three or four people in there. At least that was all Jack could see in the dark.

It was the next Friday at one-thirty in the afternoon. Jack had just arrived in Victoria. He got Johnny Merriweather, the no-voice ticket agent, to look after his suitcase and the Santa Claus he had wrapped in two old paper bags. Johnny told him Paul was probably at one of the theaters around the corner over on the square. That meant he was at either the Orpheum or the Palace. The Orpheum, on the south side, was showing *High Noon*. The Palace, across on the north side, had as its main feature *Hans Christian Andersen,* starring Danny Kaye in the title role.

The box office people and the ushers at both theaters knew Paul the Bus Driver and smiled happily in saying so. Jack did not know one person who did not smile when they talked about Paul. The woman at the Orpheum said it was his day for the Palace, and the usher there pointed Jack toward Paul with pleasure and without even asking for a ticket.

"What are you doing here, Mr. Master Operator Oliver?" Paul whispered to Jack when he finally recognized the man who had sat down next to him.

"I came to see you," Jack said. "How much time left in this movie?"

"Fifty-three minutes and twenty-two seconds," Paul said.

Jack looked up at the screen. Danny Kaye as Hans was singing a song about an inchworm to a bunch of kids.

"But no worry," said Paul. "I've already seen it seven times. That's progress, you see."

They walked outside to the park of tall trees and criss-crossing sidewalks and white wooden benches in the middle of the square.

"I almost didn't know you without your uniform," Paul said as they walked. "This may be the first time in history I have seen you like that, all naked like that in ordinary-man clothes."

Jack was wearing jeans and a light-blue and white striped short-sleeve shirt and black cowboy boots. Jack felt worse than naked here now with Paul in the clothes of a man who was no longer a bus driver. An ordinary man.

Without discussing it, they sat down on a bench by a white frame bandstand. Jack had heard about concerts and politicians' speeches there but he had never been to one. He had never been anywhere in Victoria except the bus station. Lem Odum, the retired Rosenberg teacher who wouldn't ever shut up, told Jack once that Sam Houston actually made a campaign speech there in the square when he was running for governor or senator or something in the late 1800s. Jack didn't know whether to believe him or not, although he knew for a fact that Allan Shivers, the present governor, had done that. Johnny Merriweather and a couple of others from the station had walked over and heard him. Johnny said Shivers talked mostly about why he, a Democrat, supported Eisenhower over Stevenson for president in 1952 and planned to do it again forever.

Jack tried to imagine Sam Houston standing up there on the bandstand in front of a crowd making a speech, but he couldn't. He had never seen a good picture of Houston and had no idea what he looked like.

Jack wanted to make a speech to Paul. He wanted to start shouting and never stop. He wanted to point and punch and cry about what had happened. About those two people he had run over with #4107 during the Indianola. About the deal he had made at the Hotel Surf. To go away.

Mr. Madison and all of you people of Victoria and of Texas and of the world! Listen to me! I, Jack T. Oliver, have come before you here today on this bandstand to tell you that I am a killer of a little girl and her mother. And now I am going away and away and away. . . .

He had never made a real speech before. At least not since the one about the inventor of Scotch tape in high school, unless you counted those he made to the passengers at the beginning and end of each run and at major rest stops like Victoria. Nobody would count those.

So he just started talking the regular way he always did to Progress Paul Madison.

"Sorry about the movie," Jack said.

"Like I said, this was number eight." Paul pointed to the south toward the Orpheum. "I'm up to nine on *High Noon.* They both change on Monday and I'll start again."

Jack shrugged or frowned or indicated somehow to Paul that all of that sounded terrible.

"Don't wail for me, Jack," Paul said. "The life on a daily turnaround puts me in my own bed every night. That's what's important."

"I could not see any movie eight or nine times. Isn't there anything else to do around here on the layover?"

"Not much else that I like to do. Look, they let me into

these movies for free, for one thing. You didn't come up here in civilian clothes on a day when you should be driving a bus to talk to me about watching movies on my layovers, for another. What in the hell is going on with you, Jack? You haven't been on your runs, I figured you for sick or something. Nobody seemed to know anything. The rumor machine hasn't gotten turned way up yet on you like it did on Sunshine."

What did Sunshine do? Later Jack would ask about Sunshine. Jack had come to Victoria to tell Paul Madison what in the hell was going on with him, Jack T. Oliver. And it wasn't that he was sick or something.

"Those two people who were killed during the storm down by Refugio?" he said.

"Sure. About a week ago."

"Pharmacy and Mr. Glisan think I killed them. They think I backed over them and then drove off like a hit-and-run driver."

Paul said, "That was sure some bad storm. Almost an Indianola, if the truth were known. I barely made it back to San Antone that night." Progress Paul Madison closed his eyes and shook his head. "Judas priest, Jack."

"They were checkers."

That got Paul's eyes back open. "Who were checkers?"

"The dead woman and the girl."

"Both of them?"

"Both."

"How do you know that?"

Jack told of his first meeting at the Corpus bus depot with Mr. Glisan and Rex Al Barney.

Paul again closed his eyes, shook his head and said, "Judas priest, Jack."

Then he said, "Tell me again what they looked like, how old they were and everything."

Jack didn't want to but he quickly described what little he could remember about the two people he saw lying on the highway shoulder.

Paul said, "They sound like a pair I picked up between Cuero and Thomaston last week. I hauled them here to Victoria. The woman had a twenty-dollar bill. They didn't look like checkers to me. They must be the ones who got Sunshine, too. That's progress, you see. But go on."

Jack had only one more place to go. And that was to describe a deal he was offered by Mr. Glisan, Pharmacy and Mr. Peck from the detective agency. He told Paul about the meeting at the Hotel Surf and the movie projector and the photograph.

"The detective guy said they might lose their license if it got out they were using kids under sixteen as checkers. The law says they must be over sixteen. He said they didn't know until after she died that this kid was only fourteen. Glisan said Great Western Trailways was also not keen on the whole world knowing that one of its buses had run over a couple of people and killed them. So if I would go quietly, they would stay quiet."

"In other words, they can't prove anything against you?"

"In other words, yes."

"Judas priest."

"I took the deal. I have gone quietly."

"To where?"

"I'm not sure."

Jack looked at his watch. "I want to go over and watch my old schedule come in from Houston," he said, standing up.

Paul got on his feet too. "Did they work on you to confess?"

"Yes. But I didn't."

"What about the woman passenger, the witness they found?"

"She didn't see anything, I guess."

"The movie?"

"It must not have come out or they didn't have one in the first place. They wouldn't show it to me, so that must mean they were bluffing about something having to do with it."

"I hear they had real good movies of Sunshine," Paul said.

They started walking toward the bus depot.

"How come you came up here to tell me all of this?" Paul asked.

"I had to tell somebody, and you're the closest thing to a Kenny in Kingsville I have."

"Well, well. I don't know what that means and I don't think I get it and I am not sure I am so glad you told me but that is that and here we are and that is progress, you see."

Paul pointed toward the bandstand, which was several yards off to the right of where they were walking. "You ever play a musical instrument, Mr. On Time Master Operator Oliver?"

"Nope. You?"

"The piano. I played the piano when I was in the seventh grade. I played it a whole year and loved it and then quit."

"Why?"

"I kept getting my fingers stuck down in between the keys."

Jack laughed. "I'm going to miss you, Progress."

"Nobody misses bus drivers except other bus drivers."

"Are you a Communist?"

Paul reached over and slammed his right fist against Jack's right shoulder. "Those are fighting words, Jack."

"College told me Communists want bus drivers and other people like us to run everything in Austin and Washington and the world."

"College is a stupid man who doesn't know it. They're the worst kind."

"He knows it. He told me himself he was stupid or he wouldn't be driving a bus like Sunshine and me."

"See what I mean?"

Jack didn't but it didn't matter. They were almost to the door to the bus depot.

"Was the woman in the photograph the one you had the hotsie-totsies for?" Paul said.

"Yes, sir."

"Didn't I warn you about them White Widows? Sunshine thought he had himself one, too."

Jack didn't even have to ask about Sunshine.

Paul just told the story. "You know on that Port Lavaca–Victoria turnaround he'd make four round trips a day from here to there and back. Every once in a while, it turns out, he would pay his kid brother, who worked at a gas station, to dress up in one of his extra driver's uniforms. At Bloomington, the first town out of Victoria, Sunshine would disembark and the kid brother would take over and drive the schedule on to Port Lavaca, do the layover, and then drive it back to Bloomington. Sunshine would then get back on and take the bus on into Victoria like nothing had happened. What *had* happened, of course, was that Sunshine had a couple of hours in the layover sack with the White Widow wife of the junior high school football coach. Let that be another lesson to you, too, young Mr. Oliver."

"Don't fool with wives of football coaches?"

"You're right, because they want to call all the plays and that's progress, you see."

Jack grabbed Paul's right hand and shook it hard. If Paul had been a woman he would have hugged him.

"Did they let you keep your gold badge?" Paul asked.

"Nope. I turned it in this morning to Sweet Jennings. They said it was company property, not mine."

Paul reached up to his own uniform cap and pulled it off of his head. "Here, I'll give you mine."

"No, Paul. No! You can't do that."

Paul undid the little screws that held the badge on the front of the cap. "I'll tell them some dirty rotten thief stole mine. They'll give me another one."

The badge came off in his right hand and he thrust it at Jack. "You earned this," Paul said.

Jack took it, admired it and put it in a trouser pocket. "If I was a girl I'd cry," he said, as Paul turned around and headed back toward the Palace Theater.

—

There was no guarantee, of course, that she would be there, that she would ever go again on a Friday afternoon on the bus from Victoria to Corpus Christi.

If she did come, if she was there, he would not try to talk to her inside the depot. He had already decided that. He would wait until her bus got the first call, until she came outside into the loading-docking area and got in line.

That was where he waited, with his head down. He was not interested in talking to the extra-board man who would be driving his old schedule, or to Willie Church, the porter, or to anyone else. Johnny Merriweather knew he was around but he would be busy inside the depot, handling things for the schedule.

Out of uniform, Jack was some guy waiting for a bus. Everyone else had the same problem Paul did in recognizing him as Jack T. Oliver, Master Operator.

The ACF-Brill IC-41 on Schedule 726, his schedule, pulled into the driveway nine minutes late. Jack was delighted to see that this rookie guy off the extra board, Billy McDougal, couldn't drop in from nowhere and pull his old schedule on time.

You'll never do it like I did, Billy! he wanted to shout.

Jack was also happy to see the bus was #4101, one of his favorites. She had tight brakes, soft-shifting gears and great pickup from a dead start. He felt good about seeing her now, probably for the last time.

Just under ten minutes later the awful voice of Johnny Merriweather came screeching through the PA loudspeaker. "May I have your attention, please! This is your first call for Great Western Trailways Silversides Air-Conditioned Thruliner to Corpus Christi and the Rio Grande Valley, now leaving from lane one for Inairi, Vidauri, Refugio, Woodsboro . . ."

There she was. My God, my God. There she was!

Jack moved over to her.

"Hello," he said.

She turned her head toward him. "Hello."

"Do you know who I am?"

She smiled pleasantly. The blue eyes were fully visible and exciting. "You do look familiar but I can't really place you exactly . . . I'm so sorry."

"I'm Jack T. Oliver."

It was obvious that was still not enough.

He cleared his throat and said: "Good afternoon, folks. Our travel time to Corpus Christi this afternoon will be two hours and thirty-four minutes. My name is Oliver. Jack T. Oliver. If I can assist you in any way or do anything to make your trip more comfortable, please give me a holler . . ."

"Oh, yes," she said. She did not smile.

"I'm the regular driver of this schedule."

"I see that now."

"I've been the one behind the wheel four of your five trips on this schedule. You rode across from me a week ago in the front seat. We call it the Angel Seat."

"I know I did." Her voice was no longer pleasant. She turned her blue eyes away from him, toward the door of the bus. There were still four passengers ahead of her, each having his or her ticket punched by Billy, each being helped aboard the bus.

She took a step forward. Jack moved with her.

"I'll never see you again," he said, in a voice that he hoped was low enough for no one else to hear. But he really did not care that much right now if anybody did. The important thing to him, the only important thing to him, was that she hear his every word.

She kept her eyes straight ahead and said nothing.

Jack noticed for the first time what a majestic nose she had, how magnificent she looked from the right side. He had seen mostly her left side when she was in the Angel Seat a week ago. There was something familiar about her right side. It took him a second to figure out why. He had just seen a similar profile in the lobby of the Orpheum on a poster for *High Noon.*

Ava had a profile like Grace Kelly.

She was now the next one in line to give her ticket to Billy McDougal and board the bus.

"You've given me the most wonderful times and memories of my life," Jack said to her. "I wanted you to know that before we parted for good."

"You ran over those people, didn't you?" she said. "You killed that woman and her daughter." Her expression, at least as viewed from the right side, did not change.

"Good afternoon, ma'am," Billy said to her, to Ava.

She handed him her ticket. He looked at it, at her and then at Jack, the man standing next to her.

"Jack? Is that you, Jack?" he said.

"Hi, Billy."

"Well, well. What are you doing here? Checking to see that I don't screw up the schedule? They held me for a Shreveport connection, that's why I'm late . . ."

Billy handed the passenger stub of the ticket back to her, to Ava. Then he took her left elbow, which was fully exposed below a short-sleeved green and white flowered blouse, and assisted her up the first step onto the bus.

Jack watched her take the first step with her left foot and leg and then the second with her right. And then she was gone, out of his sight down the aisle to a seat.

"Good-bye," he said quietly. "Good-bye, my love."

"Hey, Jack," said Billy. "You all right?"

Jack nodded and walked away. He had been delighted to see and now to know forever that the bump, the bite, was still gone from the calf of her right leg.

———

He went back inside the depot to get his suitcase and the Santa and to buy a ticket. But to where? What bus would he actually get on now? What did it matter anyhow?

But it did matter. He had to go somewhere.

She didn't know me. She didn't even remember my name. She thinks I ran over that woman and her daughter.

I *did* run over that woman and her daughter, that woman checker and her daughter checker, that Tamale woman and her Tamale daughter, that Fort Worth cop's wife and daughter.

Mr. Abernathy, his suitcase on the floor beside him, was talking to Johnny Merriweather.

"There won't be another one going to Panama City, Florida, until five-fifteen," Johnny said to Mr. Abernathy.

"I hate to wait that long," Mr. Abernathy said. "But if I must, I must."

"Do you know who I am, Mr. Abernathy?" Jack said, coming up to him.

Mr. Abernathy looked at him only for a second and then quickly looked away in obvious embarrassment.

"I'm Jack Oliver. That's my regular run to Corpus that just left here. Look at me closely. You'll see it."

Mr. Abernathy was clearly confused, annoyed, scared. "Where is your uniform and your punch and your bus if you are him?" he said.

"I quit, packed my suitcase just like you and decided to go off somewhere on the bus. Not as a driver but as a passenger, just like you."

Mr. Abernathy grabbed his suitcase. He obviously did not want to talk about this any more.

"Do you want to go with me?" Jack asked. "I will go anywhere you want to go."

"I was going to Panama City, Florida. I want to go to Panama City, Florida."

"Great. I'll go with you on the five-fifteen. We'll change in Houston and go to New Orleans and Mobile and then to Panama City," Jack said, turning to Johnny. "Isn't that the route?"

"That's it," Johnny said.

"What do you say, Mr. Abernathy?" Jack said.

"It's only four o'clock now," said Mr. Abernathy. "I'll be back after a while." He moved toward the door with his suitcase.

"In case I don't see you anymore, Mr. Abernathy . . ." Jack ended his sentence there.

Mr. Abernathy stopped, put his suitcase down and turned back to Jack. "I said I would be back at five-fifteen," he said sternly.

"I know, I know. I thought just in case you didn't make it,

that I would say good-bye for good, because I'm going even if you don't."

"Where are you going even if I don't go to Panama City?"

"I don't know."

"Go to Charlottesville, Virginia. Go to Thomas Jefferson's house. It's called Monticello. Go there."

"Are you sure he wasn't a Communist?" Johnny Merriweather said.

"He was a Democrat!" Mr. Abernathy said.

"Same thing," Johnny said.

Jack hadn't heard that before, even at the Tarpon Inn.

The Tarpon Inn. That was another place he would probably never see or smell again. But he wouldn't miss it. At least, he didn't think he would. How can anybody know what they'll miss before they start missing it or them or they or whatever?

He would miss Ava. Now he did know that. He would miss her in a way he had never thought possible to miss an it, a them, a they or a whatever. He did know that. Even if it turned out she looked more like a Grace than an Ava, didn't even know who he was and believed he had run over that woman and her daughter.

I *did* run over that woman and her daughter!

When he looked again at the door, Mr. Abernathy and his suitcase were gone.

Johnny Merriweather said to Jack: "Okay, now what can I do for *you*?"

"Let me think," Jack said.

"Anything you say, 'Mr. Abernathy,' " said Johnny.

———

Jack's plan when he left Corpus had been to switch to Texas Red Rocket Motorcoaches at Victoria after talking to Paul and, if possible, speaking a few parting words to Ava. Great Western was no longer a part of his life and the sooner he got it out of his life and soul the better. But that meant getting off Great Western and its glorious ACF-Brills onto a Red Rocket thirty-three-passenger Beck, a plain flat-nosed bus with a second-rate pusher engine that whined and groaned like an old Chevy. Jack had driven a few in his early days on the extra board and did not care for them. They had a high road-failure record and were hard to hold on the road in heavy winds.

He had thought he would take the 4:45 Red Rocket from Victoria to Austin, where he would transfer to a Greyhound. Then buy a ticket to Dallas and maybe as far as Kansas City. Or go on to Minneapolis. Jefferson Lines was headquartered in Minneapolis. Jefferson was one of the major independent companies in the Midwest. He had met a Jefferson driver two years ago on a charter in Corpus and he said they were good people to work for. They might want the services of a real Master Operator. Pharmacy and Mr. Glisan had promised to give him good references. That was part of the deal. He goes quietly, no charges, no noise, no repercussions, no problems.

But he might try for a job as a dispatcher or as a ticket agent. No, forget that. If he was going to do anything at all having to do with buses, he would have to drive them. He would not give up driving for Ava, so why do it now for nobody, for nothing?

There was time to work that out. It wasn't written down in Heaven or somewhere that he had to be in buses. There were other things to do in Minneapolis or somewhere.

No, no. It had to be buses. It had to be driving buses. It had to be out there on the road somewhere in some bus. It had to be.

They might also like his Santa Claus and his Christmas

decorating abilities in Minnesota. Maybe he could get a job going around decorating people's houses and yards. No, no. It had to be buses.

Hey, Mr. Abernathy! Come with me and we'll go where there are buses named after Thomas Jefferson, who was a Democrat and not a Communist. I'll drive them, you ride them. Okay? Will that do?

Minneapolis, like all the places he was thinking about, was somewhere he had never been and knew of only from some travel brochures he had occasionally glanced at. It was up north, where it was cold and there was snow and there were no beaches. No beaches at all, he was sure. So even before he got to Victoria that morning he had begun to think that maybe he would turn east at Dallas and go to one of the Carolinas, instead of north to Minneapolis. Both Carolinas were supposed to have great beaches. So was California. He would decide all of that when he got to Dallas.

In six Fridays he had gone from being a regular bus driver to being a Master Operator, something College called an "elite," to being a nothing who didn't know where he was going or what he was doing, another Mr. Abernathy.

What about Panama City, Florida? Weren't there beaches there? Charlottesville, Virginia, surely didn't have any there by Jefferson's house.

He had said good-bye to Loretta only in a note. He didn't try to explain anything; he just said he was leaving. He could not have explained it to her. He left with only a few hundred dollars from their savings, some clothes in a suitcase and Oscar the Santa. The rest, he told her in the note, was all hers. That meant the car and the house, the manger set and all the other Christmas decorations.

He could not explain it to himself, much less to Loretta.

Now he wasn't sure about going through Austin and all the rest. Where else was there to go?

And through the door came Mr. Abernathy again.

"I'll go with you if you'll go to Charlottesville, Virginia," he said to Jack.

"It's a deal," Jack said.

"What time does it go?" Mr. Abernathy asked Johnny Merriweather.

"Four forty-five, through Austin. Then to Dallas, Texarkana, Memphis, Nashville, Knoxville, Roanoke and then across to Charlottesville."

"I'll be back," Mr. Abernathy said and he left again.

"One way to Charlottesville, Virginia," Jack said to Johnny.

"You serious?"

"As life itself, Johnny," Jack replied.

—

He had told Ava, his White Widow, that she had given him the most wonderful times and memories of his life. It was true. But how could anyone ever believe or even begin to understand that.

How could anyone ever believe or even begin to understand that it was worth it to him. It was worth everything, and that included no longer being a Master Operator for Great Western Trailways. The moments he spent with her, with Ava, the experiences he had with and about her, were the best he had ever had with any woman, with any person.

He closed his eyes and was with her again.

I understand why you had to act the way you did at the bus just now, dearest.

Thank you for being so understanding, Jack dearest. It was my way of showing my love.

We were not to be, were we?

No, dearest.

Do you like decorating the outside of your house at Christmastime?

I like whatever you like, dearest.

Can we make love now?

Certainly, dearest.

They were lying side by side in the sand. Now he rose up and glided his body on top of hers. He kissed her hard on the mouth and took her head in his hands and stroked her hair.

What is your name? he asked.

Grace, dearest. My name is Grace.

He undid the first two buttons on her purple and white flowered blouse and kissed her gently.

I love you, Grace.

"Hey, Jack!" yelled Johnny Merriweather. "Your bus is about to leave!"

"*My* bus? I don't have a bus anymore . . ."

"The four forty-five, the one to Austin and on to Charlottesville. Come on, Jack. Wake up. Wake up, wake up."

Wake up, wake up. Mr. Abernathy had not come back.

"I can't leave without Mr. Abernathy," Jack said in a voice that Johnny Merriweather could barely hear.

"He isn't coming. You know that, Jack."

Yeah, Jack knew that. Jack knew that all right.

Jack stayed right there in his waiting-room seat, just like Mr. Abernathy had done hundreds of times. The bus was called, but he didn't answer the call.

He had to go home. He had to go the other way. He had to go home to Loretta.

After the bus left, he turned his ticket back in to Johnny Merriweather and bought a cheaper one, a one-way to Corpus Christi on the 6:20, College's schedule.

———

College made him sit in the Angel Seat of his bus, #4203, which Jack knew had a perpetual rattle on the left side, just above the dual tires, which no one had ever been able to fix.

"I hear it," he said to College a few blocks out, on Moody, toward Inairi.

"It's the ghost of Mr. Brill," said College.

"You really were right the other day when you said you were as stupid as me."

College grunted and kept to his driving, which Jack appreciated. They didn't say more than a handful of nothing words to each other the entire two-hour trip. College clearly knew Jack was through with Great Western—everybody knew that. But he did not say anything, which Jack appreciated for a while but then didn't. This man is not my friend. Friends care about why something as huge as what happened to me happened. He doesn't know I won't tell him. Why doesn't he at least ask? Why doesn't he say, "Hey, Jack, what happened?"

Jack did not get off the bus at any of the stops, and he got College to promise not to say anything to any agents along the way about his being on the bus. He particularly did not want to have to see or say anything to Adele Lyman in Refugio.

But he thought about her. He thought about what it must have been like for her when her husband died and she had to understand and accept the fact that he was never going to be with her again. He thought about Adele when he thought that same thing about his Ava.

He closed his eyes and kept them closed when the bus drove up to, through and away from the intersection of Highway 77 and Farm Road 682, 1.3 miles east of Refugio. He had avoided it altogether coming up the other way this morning by taking a San Antonio bus to Mathis and changing to the Laredo–Victoria bus.

The terrible part of having the imagination and the remembering mind he had was that he saw the faces of that woman and her daughter as clearly as he did the face of his Ava under him in the sand at Padre. And he knew he always would. That would be part of his life forever.

—

Loretta would never understand, but she would forgive him. They could take up their lives again the way they were before Ava and the woman and her daughter came into his. Loretta had no other place to go, no other life to lead. Neither, as it turned out, did he. He would go along with her on one thing, though. He would go along with finding a newer and better Santa than Oscar.

To Oscar, still wrapped in paper in the seat next to him, he said, "Sorry, Oscar. We'll keep you but you just won't be the star anymore."

He really might even get another job behind the wheel of a bus right out of Corpus if Mr. Glisan and Pharmacy kept their part of the deal and Slick and the highway patrol stayed in the dark. Missouri Pacific Bus Lines or Rio Grande Coaches might hire him. Missouri Pacific ran GMCs, which were all pushers and noisy but not too bad. Rio Grande Coaches carried mostly Tamales and ran mostly Fitzjohns, which were tinny like Becks, and Aerocoaches, which were called bugeyes by the drivers because the design of their front windshields resembled the wide-open eyes of bugs. Eventually he might put in an application to Greyhound. It might be something special to drive one of their new model Scenicruisers everyone was talking about. The rumors were that they were going to be deck-and-a-half luxury coaches with gigantic diesel engines, full power steering and even restrooms. The ultimate bus was what they said it would be, but that's what everybody said about every new bus that was brought out.

The main thing Jack didn't like about the idea of the ultimate bus was the automatic transmission they always said would be in them. He couldn't imagine driving a bus and not changing the gears—four speeds up, four speeds down. He couldn't imagine not double-clutching as he worked that gearshift lever up and across and back and around.

But that's progress, you see.

—

College wanted Jack to come into the Corpus depot and into the drivers' ready room with him. "I'll do my paperwork and then maybe we can get a cold one at the Tarpon and I'll drive you on home afterward," he said.

"I'll take a rain check on that," Jack said. There was no way Jack was going into the depot or the Tarpon. He had already seen and been seen by too many people since his life with Great Western Trailways came to an end, and he needed to get on with his life without it, whatever exactly it was going to be. And he needed to get home to Loretta and get on with his life with her, whatever exactly *that* was going to be.

Jack, the first passenger off the bus, followed College down the bus stairwell and, after a quick so-long salute, broke away at a slow trot toward his regular N.T.C. stop over at Lancaster and Chaparral. A bus—a blue-and-white GMC TDH37—was pulling away as he came up from the rear.

"Was that the Alameda–Staples?" he said to an elderly Tamale woman who was standing there, obviously waiting for another bus.

"Yes, yes," she said. "Alameda–Staples."

Jack knew it would be at least ten minutes before another Alameda–Staples came. He couldn't talk to this woman for ten minutes. But he couldn't just stand there doing nothing.

He would think. He would think about something pleasant for ten minutes.

His mind went to Ava, to her elbow, to her right leg. No! No, no, no. No more Ava. No more Grace. No more of that. He tried to see himself again behind the wheel of an ACF-Brill. But it was raining and then he saw those two dead people, the mother and the daughter, with blood all over and around them and in the rainwater. They both looked just like this woman at the bus stop.

Loretta. I will think about Loretta. I will imagine eating meat loaf with her like it was Friday night and then going into the bedroom. Yes, that is what I will think about. My old life returns like nothing has happened.

But something had happened. He had killed two people and he had been fired from his job and position as a Master Operator and he had run away. Now he had run back. Now he was back and everything would be the same again.

It was twelve minutes before his bus came. The driver, a guy named Shrimper Adams, didn't recognize Jack out of uniform, so it meant he would have to pay the fare. It was just as well. Jack didn't want to talk to him. He put a dime and a nickel in the fare box. It was one of those rotary machines—the driver had to keep pushing a lever to make the coins pass on through a counter and then out through a large slot at the bottom, where the driver collected the money and put it into his own five-tube coin changer for turn-in to the company at the end of his shift.

Jack went to the rear of the bus and found a seat by a window. He saw his own reflection in the window and looked away. What if Loretta would not take him back? She would. She definitely would. She was like him. She really was. Neither had any other choice but the other. She might put the freeze on him for a while and make him pay for a while but it would work out. It would work out. He could smell and taste the meat loaf. He could feel her under him. What about a movie tonight? Anything but *Show Boat*. Or *High Noon*.

His stop was coming up. He knew it without even seeing any landmarks. He knew from the passing of time and the feel of the stops and starts.

College was standing there at the corner of Staples and Anderson Street. College. College? What in the world is he doing here? I just left him back at the bus depot. What in the world?

Jack stepped off the bus through the rear folding door.

"There's been an accident, Jack," College said. "They told me when I went inside the terminal. They'd been calling all around looking for you. I jumped in my car and sped over here right away."

An accident? Yes, there has been an accident. I know all about that accident. I backed up #4101 into and onto two female persons, two Tamale persons, and killed them. I know about the accident. I was there. Why are you telling me about the accident? Why have you sped here or whatever in your car to tell me I killed those two people? I know about the accident.

I was in the accident. I was there. I am the accident.

There was a terrible smell. Something was burning. What was burning? Where was whatever it was that was burning?

The blue-and-white N.T.C. GMC TDH3102 sped off to its next stop. Maybe that smell was from the diesel motor of that bus? No, it wasn't that. Something was burning.

Jack then noticed another man standing there, behind College. The other man stepped forward. He was in uniform. But it wasn't a Great Western Trailways uniform. It wasn't a bus driver's uniform at all. It was something else. He had a holster on his right hip, but not for a ticket punch. There was a pistol in that holster. This man was not a bus driver. He was something else.

"I'm Captain Rhodes of the Corpus police," said the man. That was it. He was wearing a police uniform. Light-blue shirt, dark-blue pants, white cap. Was he causing the peculiar smell? No, no. It was a burning smell. Something was burning.

"There's been a fire at your house, Mr. Oliver," said Captain Rhodes.

Jack took off toward his house. College and the police captain were right there on each side of him.

"Fire?" Jack said. "What kind of fire?"

"A bad one, Mr. Oliver," said the police captain.

The burning smell was his house. They rounded the corner and there was his house. Some smoke was coming out of the roof. But the house was still there. There was no flame. There were several fire trucks and firemen in the street and in the front yard. A lot of other people were standing around, too.

Who are all of these people?

"Maybe we should stop right here for a minute, Jack," College said. "Let the captain explain what's happened . . ."

Yes, yes. Let's stop right here for a minute. Let the captain explain what's happened.

The captain explained: "Your wife, Mr. Oliver, was in the house. The firemen got here too late to do her any good. She's dead, Mr. Oliver."

She's dead, Mr. Oliver?

"There are some signs that it might not have been an accident, Mr. Oliver."

Not an accident?

"She was found with strings of Christmas lights wrapped around her. They began around her neck and went around her chest and under her arms and around her stomach. We don't know if she did it herself but it looks that way. It looks like she might have just wrapped those lights around herself and then walked over to an outlet, sat down on the floor and stuck the plug in the socket. She was burned pretty badly."

She was burned pretty badly.

"The fire probably started from the lights. Looks like they shorted out or something. Maybe you can help us figure it out."

I warned her about those old lights. I told her that might happen. I told her those lights were bad. I told her to throw them out.

"One of the firemen found this in a baking dish in the kitchen," said the captain. He handed Jack a folded piece of paper.

"Was it brown?"

"What?"

"The baking dish."

"Yes, I think so. Why?"

"It was what she always baked the meat loaf in."

Jack unfolded the piece of paper and read: "It's all right for you, Jack, but not for me, Jack." The words were written in black ink in Loretta's small, tight, perfect handwriting.

"She was holding another note in her right hand," said Captain Rhodes. "Unfortunately that was where the short was and most of it burned up—she may have even planned it that way. It was a note from you, Mr. Oliver."

Yes, a note from me, Mr. Oliver. A note that said that I was leaving her and Corpus and that she should go on without me.

Jack blinked his eyes and his mind. "Where is she?" he said.

"At Nueces County Hospital," said the captain. "She was pretty much gone, but they took her there to see if something could be done, but there wasn't anything. We got the word back here awhile ago that she had expired. Do you have a minister?"

Nueces County Hospital. They took her to Nueces County Hospital to see if something could be done.

"We don't have a minister," Jack said.

"What about some family or some close friends? We could take you to them afterward."

Jack looked at Oscar, who was still there under his left arm, and at College, who was still there on his right side.

There was nobody else to take him to.

"Afterward?" Jack said.

"We're going to want you to identify her, if you don't mind, Mr. Oliver," the police captain said. "I regret very much putting you through this, but there is no other way to do it.

"Texas law requires an ID from somebody who is related to or knows the deceased very well."

What does Texas law require from Master Operators who cause the deaths of wives they are related to and of checkers they don't know at all?

Jack grabbed Oscar by his right leg and threw him as hard and as far as he could toward the house and walked away with College and Captain Rhodes.

———

He saw only Loretta's neck and head; the rest of her body was covered by a white sheet. Most of her hair had been singed off and the skin on her face was coarse red and flaked. Her eyes were closed. There was a dark black ring burned deeply into and around her neck where the string of Christmas lights must have been. It was as if she had been branded by some crazy cowboy.

Jack knew he would spend the rest of his life seeing that

black branded ring and that red face and that sparse head of hair most every time he closed his eyes. If he ever closed them again, that is.

There was an insurance adjuster and an undertaker waiting for Jack when he stepped back out into the hospital hallway. The adjuster, a guy in a brown suit, about thirty-five, told him that most of the fire damage was in the kitchen, where "your missus did it." He said there was mostly smoke damage elsewhere, and that it wouldn't take somebody too much elbow grease to clean it up. He gave Jack forty-five dollars in cash to spend a few nights away at a hotel of his choice. Jack told the adjuster that he was through with the house forever, and the insurance company could do whatever it wanted to do with it. Someday he would call or write to tell them where to send whatever money there was from it all.

"I never had anybody just walk away from a house like that before," said the adjuster. "I'll have to check out what to do."

Jack didn't catch the name of the adjuster but he did the undertaker's. Morton F. Harper, Jr., of Harper and Sons. He was younger than the adjuster but his suit was darker and he had less hair. Morton F. Harper, Jr., said he was in a position to take "possession of the departed" and to "formulate and facilitate the full and final arrangements for her departure both from here at this hospital and from here on earth."

Jack told him that would be all right and he gave Morton F. Harper, Jr., the name of Loretta's parents and their phone number over at Ingleside. He also told him about Alice Armstrong, the All-American Girl.

"I've got to go now," Jack then said to the undertaker, the adjuster, Captain Rhodes and College, who had not said a word to Jack since they left the house for the hospital with Captain Rhodes.

Jack walked out the Buford Street side of the hospital and headed north and west, through downtown toward the bay, the water. He had nothing in his mind except the funeral Harper and Sons would "formulate and facilitate" for Loretta. Jack had already been to that funeral. He had gone there in his mind the afternoon he first thought about Loretta's dying. He would not go again.

He would not go again.

He came to the corner of Buffalo and Upper Broadway. There above the street, in flashing blue and white neon, was a running greyhound dog. It was the Greyhound bus depot.

He would not go again.

CHAPTER 12

*T*here he was, nine months and five days later.

Jack left Pica Chama on time but after only twenty miles and two stops he was twenty-five minutes late.

"Has there ever been one of you to get here when you were supposed to?" asked the angry woman. She was the only passenger waiting for his schedule at San Juan, this tiny town with less than five hundred people, one school, two churches, a café-tavern and a Skelly Oil station where the bus stopped. It wasn't a regular commission agency, like the ones Adele Lyman in Refugio and others ran for Great Western, because Cannonball Coaches didn't have official bus depots. They had no places with small porcelain signs hanging out front that sold tickets and took in package express or gave out schedule and fare information. Passengers and express customers had to know when the bus was coming and wait at a certain place and flag it down. In San Juan that certain place was the Skelly station.

The woman passenger at San Juan was white, large, almost middle-aged and sweating in the early July sun, along with everyone else. Jack no longer called white people Dollars and blacks Blues and Mexicans Tamales. That kind of thing didn't go over well here in New Mexico. He figured it was because there were so many Indians around and the regular people—the white people—were afraid to make up nicknames for the Indians so they didn't for anybody else either.

"Sorry," he said to the woman. "Had a mechanical problem, couldn't be helped."

"Am I going to miss my connection to Albuquerque?"

"Probably."

"There aren't any wars going on now. There's no excuse for this anymore."

The woman was right. But this was a routine normal happening, a routine normal day in Jack T. Oliver's new slow-moving, awful life driving a bus for Cannonball Coaches. The breakdown this morning was caused by a leak in the air-brake hose line in this awful worn-out bus, a twenty-one-passenger Pony Cruiser. He had fixed the leak with black tape many times but it never held for long. Randy Wilkinson, the owner of Cannonball as well as a one-man real estate business in Santa Fe, would have been more than willing to buy a new hose if anybody in New Mexico or anywhere else in the world had such a thing. Pony Cruisers weren't much better new than old. They were up-front-engine hard-riders that clanked and whammed and roared and rattled and whined like an old machine shop no matter how many years or miles they had on them. Jack had always seen the Pony Cruiser as not much of a bus. Small, inexpensive to buy, cheap on gas and oil. They had done fairly well during the war because buses were scarce, and for some reason Pony Cruiser, which was headquartered in a Michigan town named Kalamazoo, was able to keep its manufacturing lines up and working. But once the war was over and GMC, ACF-Brill, Beck Flxible and Aerocoach got back into full civilian production, Pony Cruiser lost much of its business and before long was forced to close down. What they left behind was a couple hundred of these miserable little buses being operated by small bus lines around the country who had no place to turn for air-brake hose lines and other spare parts when something went wrong.

"Will you try to step on it and at least try to make my connection at Santa Fe?" the woman asked Jack as she walked past him. Jack had not gotten out of his seat and helped her on the bus. That kind of thing was not required on Cannonball. All the driver did was open the door. It was up to the passenger to get on with baggage or whatever. Cannonball also did not issue tickets. It was all cash fares. The woman handed him exact change—two one-dollar bills and a fifty-cent piece—for the one-way passage to Santa Fe.

"Yes, ma'am," he told her but he didn't mean it. He spoke to her in a listless tone that matched the way he felt and the way he slumped behind the wheel of the Pony Cruiser. "No promises, though. Trailways won't wait for the likes of us."

No promises about anything, lady. Not even that we'll make it out of this gas station before something else on this bus breaks or cracks or boils over.

He closed the bus door, revved the motor and eased the bus back out onto the gravel road, which was dusty and rutted. The engine was there under a hatch right next to him, which meant the noise and the heat were worse than they would have been had the motor been somewhere else. Great Western's ACF-Brills' motors, of course, were pancaked underneath the center of the bus, while GMC, Aerocoach, Flxible and most of the others now were pushers, with the motors in back. Beck was the only one left besides Pony Cruiser that put the motor under a hatch right up alongside the driver.

When Jack left Corpus Christi he had no intention of doing anything like what he was doing, driving a bus for Cannonball Coaches. He had no intentions at all. He had simply gone inside the Greyhound depot on Upper Broadway just like a Mr. Abernathy or any regular passenger, walked up to the ticket counter and bought a ticket to Amarillo, in the Texas panhandle. Why Amarillo? No particular reason. It just came to him when the Greyhound agent asked him where he would like to go. He had no ideas about settling in Amarillo; it just seemed like a place to go, to stop and take a breath and get his bearings. He put some of the insurance adjuster's forty-five dollars on the counter and said, "One-way to Amarillo." Jack had never been out there, but he had heard from other Great Western drivers about Amarillo and the flat, dry land around it. The only other thing he knew about Amarillo was that U.S. Highway 66, what drivers from there called the Real Highway, went through there on the way to California.

He also knew there were no oceans or lakes or rivers anywhere in sight that would draw him to lie down by them and imagine. He was determined not to imagine again. His mother had been right about that. His imagination would get him in trouble. It ended up killing three people, the third being the only woman who ever loved him.

Now Jack had only vague memories of how he got where he was, which was in New Mexico, not Amarillo. He could remember few specifics of the bus trip from Corpus to San Antonio and then up through San Angelo on Kerrville Bus Company, a Greyhound affiliate, to Amarillo. He thought he remembered being on a Beck Steeliner from San Antonio at least as far as Big Spring, but maybe not. Maybe it was a TNM&O Coaches GMC PD4103 thru bus—called a pool car in the business. Kerrville's buses were blue and white; TNM&O's were black and white. The rides were also very different. Becks tended to sway from side to side. GMC's had a thrust feel to them, as if somebody in an army tank was ramming them down the road from behind.

At Amarillo, he jumped off the bus and started walking. He was immediately struck by the wide streets and the dry, blowing air, and he noticed that most of the men had light-brown dust or mud on their shoes or boots, and that there were a lot of churches on street corners. And there in front of him, after a while, was the Trailways bus depot. It was newer and fancier than the Greyhound station. The whole side of the building where the buses came in and parked was glass, and the loading docks—there were ten—were cut in like a long blade of saw teeth. Two ACF-Brills were parked at docks. One of them had LOS ANGELES on its front destination sign, the other said MEMPHIS. It was all right to go in. Nobody would know him here.

"How do you go from here to Mount Rushmore?" he asked a young ticket agent inside. He was not even tempted to tell the young man that he, Jack T. Oliver, had until five days ago been a Master Operator for Great Western Trailways, the Route of the Silversides Thruliners, which were Cheaper by Far Than Driving Your Car and were Always Going Your Way to the Next Town or Across America.

Jack watched the agent pull out the Red Guide, *Russell's Official Motor Coach Guide,* and look up the route and schedule.

"It says here that Mount Rushmore is up by Rapid City, South Dakota," said the kid agent. "Nobody's ever asked me about going there before. You could go from here up to

Denver and then to Cheyenne and on to Rapid City. Our next Denver bus is in two hours."

Jack didn't want to wait around for two hours. But he had a question. "Does it say in the guide who is the fourth president at Mount Rushmore besides Washington, Lincoln and Thomas Jefferson?"

The kid agent looked back at the book. "Theodore Roosevelt, it looks like to me from this small picture. Teddy Roosevelt. The guy with the funny glasses."

"Thanks," Jack said. Teddy Roosevelt. Right. Jack remembered his being mentioned in school but he could not remember for what.

He smiled at the agent and stepped away. The Los Angeles bus was into its last-call loading. He watched the driver tear the tickets and handle the baggage and put aboard three or four final passengers. The driver had a silver Panhandle Trailways badge on his cap. Jack fingered the gold Master Operators badge in his right pants pocket. He had put it there when Progress Paul Madison gave it to him and he had not gone anywhere without it since.

Jack walked through the glass door to the Los Angeles bus. He flashed his badge to the driver, who invited Jack to come along with him "as far as you want to go." It was a technical violation of the rules, because an off-duty driver also was supposed to show his annual pass and do some paperwork in order to ride a Trailways bus. Jack had turned in his pass with his own badge when he was suspended.

Jack climbed aboard and took the Angel Seat, and it wasn't long before they were headed west out on the straight flat concrete of U.S. Highway 66 toward Tucumcari, Albuquerque and points west. *The* U.S. Highway 66. Jack had heard drivers talk about Highway 66 and he had thought and wondered about it, but he had never "taken bottoms over it," as one of the Houston–Beaumont drivers used to refer to driving a bus of passengers on a particular road or highway.

This Amarillo driver was a quiet, soft-spoken man—he said they called him Chatter because he didn't talk much— who told Jack he had been with Panhandle Trailways for eleven years, driving mostly Amarillo–Albuquerque and Amarillo–Oklahoma City overnights since he graduated off the Amarillo extra board. He asked Jack where he was headed and why he was in Amarillo. Jack made it up as he went along, saying he was not headed for anyplace in particular and had just taken some time off to see a little of the country. One day this man would probably find out that the guy he gave a free ride to because he thought he was a Master Operator was really none other than that awful Jack T. Oliver man down in Great Western's South Texas Division who killed all those people—including his own wife.

As the bus hummed down the open road, Jack suddenly wanted to jump out and off. It was too much. The memories were too ferocious, too terrible, but also, the hummier it got out there on the open road, they were also too wonderful. He simply could not bear sitting there in the Angel Seat, watching this other man drive this Trailways ACF-Brill. He wanted off this bus, out of this world.

That was why he got off in a place called Clines Corners, New Mexico, a good thirty miles short of Albuquerque. The other major reason was that an orange and yellow Flxible Clipper, like the one Paul Madison drove on his Victoria–San Antonio turnaround, was waiting there at the small café where the buses stopped. Chatter said the Flxible had come from Roswell to the south and was now on its way north to Santa Fe. Sometimes we have connecting passengers for it, he told Jack.

How about me being the connecting passenger this time? I have to get off this bus!

And within minutes Jack was in the Flxible on his way to Santa Fe. The bus line that owned and operated the bus was called Land of Enchantment Stages, and the driver said they were mostly a feeder line from the smaller cities and towns of New Mexico to both Trailways' and Greyhound's competing main east–west and north–south lines. Jack decided then and there that he wanted to go to work for Land of Enchantment Stages, but the driver said he would have to go the other way, to company headquarters in Roswell, to apply for a job. He also said they weren't hiring right then because business had really been falling off lately, like it was for everybody in the bus business.

Fate and Randy Wilkinson, owner of Cannonball Coaches, intervened. Wilkinson was at the Santa Fe bus depot with his terrible little Pony Cruiser and a terrible problem. His only driver had just walked off the job. Jack showed him his gold Master Operator badge, and after thirty minutes of talk over coffee in the depot café, Jack T. Oliver became a driver for Cannonball Coaches.

That was nine months and five days ago. Now here he was trying to get that awful little Pony Cruiser the 103 miles between Pica Chama and Santa Fe one more time. It was a route that Land of Enchantment Stages had run for years but because of dwindling business had given to Randy Wilkinson to operate. Jack made two round-trips a day, six days a week—Wilkinson's brother, a Santa Fe police officer, drove it on Mondays—leaving Santa Fe in the morning at 7:05 going north and ending up back there at 8:15 at night. That was if the Pony Cruiser did not have a problem, which, like today, it usually did.

Jack lived in a rented room in an old two-story house three

204 | JIM LEHRER

blocks from downtown and the bus depot. One reason Jack chose the place was that the two elderly women who owned the house said it was all right for him to park the Cannonball bus on the street in front at night. Jack had to share the bathroom with four other men who had rooms on the second floor, and he hated that. But that was life.

So was seldom being able to close his eyes and fall asleep in his narrow bed in his hot room before one or two in the morning.

So was seeing the faces of Loretta and/or those two Tamale checkers when he did close his eyes.

So was not wearing a tie or a long-sleeved uniform shirt or a driver's cap or a badge or a ticket punch or shined shoes or anything else he had once considered as important to being a bus driver as the bus itself.

So was not having anybody in his life with whom he could go to the movies or have a cup of coffee or a steak.

So was not having anybody even to tell last Thursday that it was his thirty-seventh birthday.

So was the thought that this was going to be the rest of his life.

The next town, Perryville, was even smaller than San Juan. All it had was a grocery store with a single Gulf gas pump and a field behind it full of wrecked and junked cars and trucks. Jack pulled up front and thought, as he did every time, that it was in that field, that graveyard back there, that this lousy bus was someday going to meet its maker.

There were no people waiting for his bus. He honked his air horn and looked around to see if anybody came running toward the bus. Nobody did.

"Can we just go on?" said the woman who wanted to make the connection to Albuquerque.

She was one of only three passengers. The other two were

Indians, both men, who got on at Pica Chama. Three passengers. In all of his years with Great Western he never drove a regular scheduled run with only three passengers.

In all of his years with Great Western he never looked like this either. He had already put thirty of his old pounds back on and he knew more were coming. He had gotten a late start this morning and didn't take the time to shave. Wilkinson didn't care and neither did anyone else. His pants were soiled khakis that he had bought at a Woolworth's in Santa Fe. His light-blue short-sleeved shirt had come from there, too. It was the second day in a row he had worn it. It had been more than a month since he'd had a haircut and his hair was down over the collar in back. Nobody cared.

He glanced up into his rearview mirror. The woman passenger was two rows back on the left side. She was over forty, at least, and she had no style or class. She was definitely no White Widow. She was definitely no Ava, no Grace. He immediately despised himself for even thinking such a thing. But it didn't really matter that much anymore. Since he had put on the weight and gotten sloppy in his dress and appearance, all thought of Ava and White Widows meant nothing. No woman in her right mind would take a second look at him now. He knew it, and knowing it kept him from imagining otherwise. There would be no more Avas in his mind and in his life to cause him to run over people and cause his wife to kill herself. It was a great relief, a great release. It was the only relief and release he had experienced but it was something, it was a beginning.

"Why won't you even try to make it?" the woman passenger barked at him. She had met his eyes in the mirror. She knew he was looking at her. "You're just poking along like we've got all day," she said.

Jack wasn't looking at her anymore.

"There ought to be a law that only lets real bus drivers drive these things," said the woman, apparently not only to Jack but to the whole world.

Jack wanted to stop and run back there and show the woman his gold badge.

Look at this, lady! I was a Master Operator. I was On Time Jack Oliver. Look at this! I was the best bus driver in the world! Almost, at least, except for Paul Madison. Look at this! I was a Master Operator!

Was?

He now had a straight shot into Santa Fe. Only two more stops, and most of the road was paved. The southbound Mesa Verde Trailways left Santa Fe for Albuquerque at 12:05. Jack glanced down at his wristwatch. That was exactly thirty-two minutes from now.

In the old days I could have made it. It would be tough and take some doing and some luck—some Master Operator luck—but I could do it.

Was?

With his right foot on the accelerator, he increased the speed a bit. He took a deep breath and let it out and moved his shoulders around as if to loosen them and him. He sat straight up in the seat and gripped the steering wheel firmly.

Then he reached down into his right pants pocket and pulled out the Master Operator badge. He felt it and peeked at it and placed it up on the dashboard in front of him.

Was?

There was a line of slow-moving traffic in front of him. He counted two cars and a pickup truck, none of them in a hurry to get anywhere.

Was?

He saw a break in the oncoming traffic in the left lane; he eased the bus into it, hit the air horn and floorboarded the accelerator. The little Pony Cruiser, rising to the occasion, took off like a jackrabbit with buckshot in its butt.

Jack, timing it perfectly, swung the bus back into the right lane several smooth seconds before an oncoming green pickup would have been a problem.

His mind and his attention and his reflexes and his muscles and his soul were all in sync now, all concentrating on moving that little bus down New Mexico State Highway 6 with a precision and grace that only the very best bus drivers in the world are capable of.

Here he was again, out on the road at full speed. On the open road at full speed.

In a few minutes Jack and his Pony Cruiser were at Cubano, another wide place in the road, where he could be flagged by people at an intersection in front of the Catholic church. He slowed the bus down and hit the air horn and watched for people. There were no trees or signs or anything else to obstruct his view. Nobody was there to catch his bus.

He gunned the bus without ever pulling off the road. At Great Western that would have been a mark-down offense, but this was not Great Western. And, besides, he had a connection to make.

And, besides, I have a connection to make.

A medium-sized truck, old and slow, pulled out in front of him five miles farther down the road. There was an incline and a curve ahead, which made passing on the left dangerous or impossible. But there was a wide gravel shoulder on the right. Jack maintained his speed and zipped that bus right up and around and in front of that truck. The driver, who looked to Jack like a Mexican, had a surprised and scared expression on his face. But it all happened so fast he didn't have time to react in a way—like suddenly pulling to the right himself—that would have endangered anybody.

The next town, a place called Lambville, was larger, with a population of more than one thousand. Here Jack had to leave the highway, turn right for a block, take a left and drive down the main street for a block, and then head back to the left to the highway. The designated flag-stop place was Lambville Rexall at the second downtown intersection. There were usually passengers here, and he saw two people with two suitcases standing in front of the drugstore as he approached. The Cannonball Coaches way of picking up passengers wouldn't be good or fast enough this time.

Jack stopped the bus, moved the gearshift into neutral, jerked back the emergency brake, opened the bus door and leaped out. He grabbed the two suitcases and came close to carrying the two passengers, an elderly Mexican couple, onto the bus himself. Less than a minute had gone by from the time he stopped the bus.

Back on the highway a few seconds later, he looked at the woman passenger in the second row on the left. She was smiling at him.

He would have smiled back but he didn't have the time to waste.

According to his watch, it was 11:53. He now had only twelve minutes left. Normally the trip into Santa Fe from Lambville the leisurely Cannonball way took Jack twenty minutes or more. That would not be good enough this morning. He had a connection to make.

I have a connection to make!

He kept the speed as high as he dared, usually ten or fifteen miles above the limit, and he geared up and down and gunned and pedaled and honked. Joe "Rocket" Ridgley would have been proud of him. He came up to a car turning left, blocking traffic from behind. He squeezed the bus by on the right, with only a few inches to spare between the bus and a drainage ditch. He crowded a yellow light at the intersection with the road from Taos. And as he entered the city limits of Santa Fe, he rolled through a stop sign without coming to a full stop.

Suddenly his imagining came back. As he turned down Smith Street in Santa Fe he saw instead Main Avenue in Houston. He felt the hum of an ACF-Brill IC-37 under him instead of the wham and whine of this Pony Cruiser. He felt he weighed 186 instead of 210. And he saw himself dressed again in starched and pressed gray, with that gold badge on his hat instead of on the dashboard. He was again, in his imagination, On Time Jack Oliver, Master Operator.

His real watch said 12:03. He was now at Water Street, only a block from the bus depot at 126 Water in the center of downtown Santa Fe, New Mexico.

You're all right, little bus, he said to the Pony Cruiser.

He whipped the little bus into the depot loading area and saw the sight he wanted to see. The 12:05 Mesa Verde Trailways southbound was sitting there. It was an ACF-Brill IC-41 Silversides Thruliner with its heavy motor running but with the door still open. Jack braked his bus to a dramatic stop right behind it, opened his bus door and yelled to the woman in the second row and his other four passengers: "Santa Fe!"

For the first time in a long time, he then got out of his seat and helped the passengers disembark.

"I've never seen anything like it," said the woman as she hurried down and off and past him. "I mean it. I wasn't sure if we were going to die or make it but it was going to be one or the other. You are a terrific bus driver. I'm sorry for what I said earlier."

Jack smiled and saluted, as if he had a cap to put his right hand to.

The woman ran toward the Trailways bus, which resembled the buses Jack drove between Houston and Corpus. The Mesa Verde Trailways driver came out of the drivers' ready room at that moment. Jack waved at him, but the Trailways man only nodded. None of the mainline drivers, Greyhound as well as Trailways, paid much attention to any of the feeder lines' drivers.

I'm as good as you, buddy! Better even!

Jack stepped back up inside his little bus and sat down behind the steering wheel. He reached down to the dashboard and picked up his Master Operator's badge. He held it tightly in his right hand and he closed his eyes,

For the first time in nine months and five days he did not see the faces of dead people.

He saw himself in full bus-driver livery, standing with Mr. Abernathy. They were looking at a mountain that had big faces of Theodore Roosevelt and three other presidents chiseled into it.

Jack looked with Mr. Abernathy back to a road where an ACF-Brill IC-37 was sitting with its motor idling. Jack knew this bus. It was #4208. She had a slight vibration at the low speeds and the steering was a bit stiff turning to the left but she was a magnificent piece of equipment.

"All aboard, Mr. Abernathy," Jack said.

"Where are you going today?" Mr. Abernathy asked.

"To the Next Town or Across America—to Inairi, Vidauri, Refugio, Woodsboro, Sinton, Odem, Calallan, Corpus Christi and the Rio Grande Valley."

"Oh my, that's too bad. I'm packed for the other direction."

"That *is* too bad. Well, then, I'll see you next time."

"Yes, that will be fine," said Mr. Abernathy. "I'll just wait here with Mr. Jefferson and the others until my bus comes."

"I always have a seat for you, Mr. Abernathy," Jack said, as he waved good-bye, climbed up into #4208 and slid into the driver's seat.

He hit the lever to close the door and looked up into the rearview mirror.

There she was. My Ava. Sitting in the fifth-row left-side window seat. She was wearing the light cream-colored blouse, the same one she had on that afternoon they first met.

She was looking out at Mount Rushmore at Mr. Jefferson, Mr. Teddy Roosevelt, Mr. Lincoln and Mr. Washington.

Your face is as beautiful from the side as it is from the front, Ava dear.

Thank you, Jack dearest.

Could you live in New Mexico, my Ava?

I can live wherever you are, my Jack.

He doubled-clutched, gently pushed the gearshift lever into first and revved the motor slightly. Then he eased up gradually on the clutch, turned the steering wheel smoothly and forcefully to the left and moved on down the road.

There, like Refugio, he was again.

ABOUT THE AUTHOR

JIM LEHRER worked as a Trailways ticket agent in Victoria, Texas, while attending Victoria College in the 1950s. *White Widow,* his tenth novel, is based on that experience. Lehrer has also written two books of nonfiction and three plays. He is the anchor and executive editor of *The NewsHour with Jim Lehrer* on PBS and lives with his wife, Kate, in Washington, D.C. They have three daughters.

A B O U T   T H E   T Y P E

This book was set in Sabon, a typeface designed by the well-known German typographer Jan Tschichold (1902–74). Sabon's design is based upon the original letter forms of Claude Garamond and was created specifically to be used for three sources: foundry type for hand composition, Linotype, and Monotype. Tschichold named his typeface for the famous Frankfurt typefounder Jacques Sabon, who died in 1580.